IN LAST NIGHT'S CLOTHES

HAYDEN WINSTON

First published in 2012, this revised edition of In Last Night's Clothes is dedicated to my parents.

Dad, thanks for always encouraging me to be better.
Manman mwen, thanks for hanging in there.

September 24, 2009

It's autumn and that's always been my favorite season. As you know, the climate doesn't change much here in Southern California, but something about the shift in seasons always invigorates me. I love how the thin, delicate, little trees lining the edges of the sidewalks, silently spill their scarlet-colored blossoms. Today was one of those days that was too gorgeous to stay in, so I went out. I strolled lightly underneath the little trees. I was dressed in a smooth black coat, navy button-down shirt, and slim-fit denim jeans. Careful to keep up with what's in trend and still retain my originality. After all, I'm Colin Prescott. My eyes are still the dark shade of chestnut, my hair – jet-black, fine, and clean cut. I'm still slender, 5'7", with the same dark brown complexion you'd remember.

However, I can't deny that things are unmistakably different in many ways since you've been gone. I'm still the perfect young gentleman you'd remember on the outside, but I've grown calloused on the inside. Why shouldn't I? Love is hell and lust is rapture. I didn't just adopt this belief out of nowhere. I have my reasons for morphing into the creature I've become. I thought I should share them with you. You were always a great listener. I guess I should start at the beginning.

It all began where it always begins with these things, at home. My parents divorced when I was in kindergarten. It was had an acrimonious. My mom, Katherine 'Kate' Lane became the primary caretaker for my older sister Traci and me thereafter. Dad claims he didn't want to fight her for custody. Maybe he just wanted to be free. Kate is a public relations assistant, who hails from the Eugène clan. The Eugènes are a prominent, old, Roman Catholic family from the island of Saint Lucia. They're firmly West Indian and yet staunchly proud of their French ancestry. Saint Lucia declared its independence from the United Kingdom in 1979.

However, the island changed hands between the British and the French a total of 14 times until 1814[1]. This contention earned it the nickname the "Helen of the West" (as in Helen of Troy). It also left behind a unique impact on St. Lucia's cultural heritage. For example, Catholicism is the majority religion on the island due to French influence, while Anglicanism follows at a close second.

Saint Lucia is both a member of the Commonwealth of Nations and La Francophonie. English is the official language of the country, but many of the place names are in French (e.g., Canaries, Gros Islet, Vieux Fort, etc.). Furthermore, Saint Lucian Creole (or Kwéyòl Sent Lisi) is widely spoken across the island and is the preferred tongue at home for many local families. Kwéyòl is a French-based creole that incorporates African and Carib languages with loan words from English, Spanish, and Portuguese. It's mutually intelligible with the creoles spoken on the nearby islands of Dominica, Martinique, Grenada, and Guadeloupe among others. I know a few words, but I can't speak it fluently. Kate never taught us. To be fair, when she was growing up the British heavily encouraged Lucians to speak the Queen's English.

Fortunately, many of the older Lucian clans (including mine) refused to let Kwéyòl die and helped continue its use into the modern day. Kate still speaks it to her family and friends back home. I've heard that my maternal great-great-grandparents primarily spoke Kwéyòl. They were free people of color of mixed French descent – a merchant and a seamstress, who became influential in post-slavery society. They ensured their children were educated and married well. A mere generation later and the Eugènes had secured their place amongst the island's elite. Countless members of that side of my family have been doctors, lawyers, professors, and architects ever since. In fact, my maternal great-grandfather, Joseph-Henri Eugène was a doctor. My great-aunt, Inès was editor-in-chief of the local newspaper.

Kate is the quintessential product of such an auspicious upbringing. She's

---

[1] The 1814 Treaty of Paris ended the war between France and the Sixth Coalition (UK, Russia, Austria, and Prussia). Saint Lucia, Seychelles, and Tobago were ceded to the UK by France as part of this treaty.

intelligent, beautiful, vain, materialistic, and not to be crossed. She can be your loving, loyal, defender, or a manipulative tyrant. It just depends on the day. As my siblings and I grew into teens, she often neglected to be there for us in favor of maintaining her social life, boosting her career, or keeping a lover. Following her divorce from my dad, she married Anderson Lane, a computer engineer from a well-off Chinese family. The Lanes first fled from China to Taiwan at the onset of the Chinese Communist Revolution.

They emigrated from Taiwan to the U.S. when Anderson was six. They claim they changed their surname from Liang to Lane to better assimilate to American culture. I suspect it was an evasive measure. Kate's marriage to Anderson lasted a decade and was disastrous to say the least. The upside was that it produced my and Traci's younger half-brother, Parker. Even though Kate and Anderson have been long divorced, they still spend some holidays together. This is supposedly for Parker's sake, but I think they're locked in some sort of toxic tango. Anyway, Traci was always Dad's favorite and Parker is our mom's favorite.

I usually call her Kate in conversation, unless I'm speaking directly to her or to one of my siblings about her. We were raised never to call adults by their first names (especially not our parents), so it feels transgressive when I do it behind her back. Growing up I resented being the middle child. I must admit I still do a bit now, but I realized as I got older that this meant I could get away with pretty much anything I wanted. No one was paying close attention. Aside from doting on the children they loved most, my parents had demanding lives of their own to lead.

My dad, Jude Prescott is a hard-working man from Barbados. His parents had him when they were both in their late teens, so he was raised by his widowed paternal grandmother. I was named Colin after his father. Sadly, I only met my namesake once at my christening. He died in a car accident during my infancy. I never met my own paternal grandmother. Cancer claimed her life while Dad was in primary school.

After primary school, Dad went to St. Croix in the U.S. Virgin Islands to live with close relatives. In St. Croix he joined the Navy, where he became a cook. He was near the end of his contract he met Kate. She had just arrived to attend nursing school at University of the Virgin Islands. Once he was out of the service, Dad proposed to her. My maternal grandparents weren't too thrilled with the match, so they made Kate choose. To their shock, she chose to abandon her comfortable life. She ran off with Dad.

They eloped and moved to California. Kate eventually dropped out of nursing school and pivoted into marketing. She said she left nursing because it was the 80s and she feared catching HIV via patient blood draws. Dad says she let a friend convince her that she could make more money in marketing, without having to work as hard as a nurse. As you can imagine, this caused a huge rift between my parents and Kate's side of the family. What happened next horrified the Eugènes more than any other scandal imaginable. Dad and Kate immersed themselves in Pan-African activism, and even adopted Garveyism. They became vegans and grew dreadlocks. They deserted all the formalities of civility Kate was raised with.

Dad tried to mend things by proving he was an upstanding citizen, but to no avail. He worked at a few odd jobs to put himself through culinary school, while Kate earned her marketing degree. My maternal grandparents finally came around when Dad and Kate had Traci (they're still not big fans of my father, but they tolerate him now). By the time I was born a few years later, Dad had risen to the ranks of executive chef at tasteful restaurant called Aquarius in West LA. Following his divorce from my mother, he bought a house, and started his life over with his new wife, Faye. Faye and I have never been fond of each other. I was 12 when we first met and made my displeasure known. I saw her as an ill-mannered, country bumpkin and she saw me as pretentious city boy.

I've since grown to suspect that Faye views Traci and me as an impediment to a truly happy life with Dad. We represent his past with another woman. One who he loved deeply at that. Kate kept us in LA so we could be near Dad, until the summer of '04, when she moved us to Villa Valle. I continued to see Dad on weekends and holidays after that, but we've never really been close. We do however share an uncanny likeness, which is no doubt a source of resentment for Kate, who frequently mentions our similarities. Dad and I also share a love of cologne, watches, and shoes. He usually gifts me one of the three on special occasions. It may sound like I had a charmed childhood, but quite the opposite is true. My parents were prudent about not spoiling us.

I knew from an early age that if I wanted something I had to suffer for it. For example, most of my peers received cellphones at the start of high school. My freshman year at Villa Valle High School, I had to beg my dad for one. When I finally got a phone, it had limited minutes. I ended up getting a job as soon as I turned 16, so I could get a plan with a contract. During my junior year at VVHS, most of my classmates' received cars from their parents (a necessity in a sprawling suburb). I, however, was made to walk and figure out the sparse bus routes. I guess Dad and Kate figured they were teaching Traci and me to be independent, but I always thought they were just being cheap.

When I turned 17, Kate sued Dad for an increase in child support. Dad counter sued for shared custody of me, and it devolved into a nasty court battle. Can you imagine two bitter exes fighting for custody of their 17-year-old? It was evident to me that Dad didn't really care about me, or he would have tried to gain custody years ago. He just didn't want to give Kate any of his hard-earned money. He bought anything I asked for and he felt that was enough. Due to my age, Kate's attorney advised that the judge would likely ask me to choose which parent I wanted to live with. I chose Kate. I figured it was better to go with the devil I knew, than the devil I was only vaguely familiar with. Kate instructed to write a letter to judge to explain my reasoning. Unfortunately, she heavily altered the contents, which deepened the schism between my father and me.

I guess can't really complain in the grand scheme of things. Without much parental oversight to get in the way, I was left free to discover everything within my grasp. By the time I was 18, I had read Angelou, Baldwin, Haley, and Walker. I was acutely aware of and unapologetic about being young, Black, and privileged. I could also definitively state that I enjoyed gin martinis, casual flings, and contemporary art.

Being left to my own devices taught me a great deal of self-reliance. Although we're different in many ways, I inherited a lot of my personality traits from my parents, as we all do. From Kate, I received my sense of style, biting wit, and my ability to persevere. From Dad, I received my inclination towards fairness and capacity for obstinance. Now that you're armed with my formative history, we can move on.

Returning to my story, it is autumn. Traci just graduated from University of California at Berkeley. Our 17-year-old half-brother, Parker has just returned home. He was attending a summer program at Julliard and is back to finish his senior year at VVHS with his old friends. And what have I been up to all summer? Well, I was supposed to be off preparing for to start school in London this fall, but Kate derailed those plans. I had an admissions interview scheduled last year. It was with a private school that was willing to consider my exceptionally high-test scores over my lack luster grades. But of course, Kate mixed up the flight times.

We arrived at the airport at 6:00 pm instead of 6:00 am. There were no alternative flights that would have gotten us there in time for the interview. I missed my shot and that means waiting a year before I can re-apply. Kate was determined to salvage the trip and made it a vacation to Jamaica instead. I couldn't get out of going as apparently my name was on the ticket. I was 16 and had just watched my biggest dream crushed before my very eyes. Meanwhile, she was busy making plans for Jamaica.

I went on the trip, and I was miserable the entire time. Who wouldn't be? When we got back, she told her friends that I was a spoiled brat, who hadn't enjoyed the trip she took me on. It was a gross oversimplification. What a funny way to twist things. I had had enough of her twisting things. Anyway, I've decided to go Villa Community College and try to transfer to a university from there in a couple years. In the meantime, I've been smoking cannabis and experimenting with Xanax most days. Most nights, I've been drinking and partying, until I passed out.

Today is a little different though. Today I decided to stay sober and have coffee with a good friend. She was waiting for me at a coffee shop, just blocks from where I walked underneath those wonderful little trees I told you about. I was late, as usual. She was tapping her fingernails against the tabletop. Her name is Lexie. I think you met her once. She's only an inch or so taller than me with shoulder-length light brown hair, a pearl-white smile, and sparkling blue eyes. Those eyes gave away all her emotions, whether it was sadness, joy, or annoyance. She was a cynic by nature. She was always joking about waiting for death. I could never tell if her suicidal ideation was authentic, or it was just a bit. Nonetheless, I appreciated not having to feign positivity around her.

As I waltzed into Café Insomnia, I spotted her immediately. Café Insomnia is our favorite coffee shop. We always sit at the exact same quaint looking table, in front of a floor to ceiling window. From that particular table, you can see Montclair Park. We often sat there and watched the sunset over the horizon. I went over to our usual spot and sat directly across from her. She already had a latte, but it appeared to be fresh. Lexie joked that it took me forever to arrive and I joked back about her impatience.

"So, what have you been up to? How's Kaitlin?" she said. Kaitlin was the girl that I'd been seeing. She wasn't officially my girlfriend yet, but we've gone on several dates and things are heading in that direction. If I didn't put a stop to it first that is. I usually avoided confining myself to the societal expectations of masculinity. Hook-up culture was the one exception. I hated it, but I was steeped in it.

"She's good," I said. I didn't want to get into it. But of course, Lexie wouldn't let me get away that easily. She knew me well and that meant she knew something was up. She poked and prodded at my response. She was often my voice of reason and vice-versa. In fact, the only time my judgment seemed sound is when I was giving her or some other friend advice. I was a sage when it came to helping others, yet practically incompetent at keeping my own affairs in order (go figure). "I think I'll have a coffee after all or maybe a chocolate croissant," I said. I was hoping to change the subject.

"You're avoiding the topic, so it can't be good."

"It's not bad," I said quickly. It almost sounded sincere, but Lexie could see right through me. I hated that. We were practically flirting before, but that banter had quickly devolved into an interrogation. The sunlight shone in through the window onto her face. I must admit she looked heavenly, even though she was holding me to task.

"What's her name?" Lexie said. She rolled her eyes as she did.

"Why do you assume it's another woman? Maybe I've taken up a new hobby."

"I know you too well, that's why." She grinned and I relented immediately.

"Alessandra," I said. I'm such a sucker for a warm smile. Of course, a name was simply not enough. Lexie asked me to describe Alessandra next. I'd been expecting her to ask a barrage of questions, but I hadn't yet thought of all the answers. I wound up saying she was indescribable, and Lexie prodded further.

"Give it a try," she said. "With that extensive vocabulary of yours, I'm sure you can find the right words." There was that sharp tongue. I loved it.

"Goddess incarnate," I said. I paused to read her face, and her expression said it all. Lexie could hardly contain her repulsion. I had to level with her. "Fine, she's tall. She has long hair, raspberry-colored lips, and hazel eyes that can appear rather menacing or sensual depending on her mood. She has a strong, yet feminine jaw, but what I adore most about her physically is her figure. She's dangerously curvy." A ravenous silence ensued and hung in the air. She had a way of speaking without saying a word. She was judging me, no doubt.

For some strange reason, I felt the need to justify myself to her. "That's not the only reason I enjoy her company, you know," I added. "She's super smart. She was the valedictorian at Sacred Heart. We share common interests in culture, documentaries, and the literature."

"Well, allow me to withdraw my cynicism then," she said. She glanced at me and took a big sip of her latte. "I forgot what a history nerd you are."

I smiled. "That and mild S&M fantasies," I said.

"And I retract my withdrawal," she said. She chuckled, then gazed out the window. After a few moments, she started again. "I think you're fascinated with Alessandra because she reminds you of Leona." She stared me directly in the eyes. Her soul reading mine. "I'm right, aren't I?"

I had gone from feeling a bit unnerved to terribly uncomfortable. I was sweating. She wasn't right. Alessandra and Leona were the exact opposites. Still, I hated that the very mention of Leona's name flustered me. I wanted out of this feeling immediately. "I think we should change the subject," I said.

"Have you even heard from her or seen her since…"

"No and I'm fine with that."

"Oh, ok."

I could tell by her reaction that I'd spoken too sternly. I paused for a second and regained my composure. "It feels like things turned out the way they were supposed to."

"Ok," said Lexie, sounding convinced at my response this time. "So, Alessandra…" she said gently. She was trying to restore the mood of the conversation. I yielded. We finished talking about Alessandra as the sun set. We decided to get up and walk down Grant Boulevard for a bit. We soaked in the warm hues of the buildings as we passed by. The light wind rustled my coat and the sheer glossy looking scarf that hung about her neck. She fiddled to keep it in place, and I noticed she was wearing an old familiar necklace.

It was a sterling silver chain with an owl pendant hanging from it. I teased her mercilessly about it in high school, but secretly thought it was kind of cool. Her sister had given it to her as a Christmas gift. It was a little trinket to remind her to always make wise choices. Lexie wore it every day after first receiving it, then one day she just stopped. I guess she ceased believing that charms and talismans could make a difference. I was never one to believe that sort of thing myself.

As a child, Kate insisted I wear silver jewelry to protect me from evil spirits. As I grew older, I abandoned that old island superstition. Lexie and I probably would have made a good couple in another life. In this life, she was searching for a reliable partner, and I was too set in my ways to be that for anyone. There's was also the fact that her parents are vehemently racist. I suppose we could have dated in covertly, but I refuse to be anybody's secret boyfriend.

Despite the improbability of us ever being an item, Lexie played games with me for a while. She'd call me in the middle of the night to talk. She'd convince me to drop girls she didn't deem worthy of me. I don't believe she had real interest in dating me herself, but she wanted me on the sidelines for a while, just in case. I pined over her, but of course I continued to see other girls. As people in odd situations tend to do, we eventually grew content with the status quo.

We both dated in rapid succession. The only difference was, she was seeking a long-term relationship, while I was enjoying the savage pleasure of non-committal life. We approached Kenmore Avenue and made small talk about increasingly cold weather and the uncanny number of people still resigned to wearing shorts and sandals. We walked up to the plush six-story building, Lexie called home. We turned to face one another. She looked at me with a mixture of hope and sympathy.

"You know, I just want you to be happy Colin," she said.

"Of course," I said.

"I'm serious," she said. I could hear the sincerity in her voice.

I smiled warmly. "I know," I said. There was an uncomfortable pause, and I made sure to break it. "Now I have to get going. School tomorrow, you know?"

"Today is Friday Colin," Lexie said as she laughed.

"I know that too," I said. I loathed being serious about things for too long. Perhaps it's a defense mechanism, perhaps it's immaturity. I don't quite know. We hugged and she walked up the short steps and into the lobby of her apartment building. I watched her go inside and began to walk away slowly. Though she was out of sight, the words she'd just spoken hung in the air with a certain kind of stillness.

"I just want you to be happy." I knew what she really meant was that she wanted me to fall in love with someone already and stop all this madness. She'd never say that though. She knew I wouldn't listen. Love was a taunt to me. Love was something that seemed so easily attainable, so straightforward, but wasn't. Love was Ahab's whale. It had lured me out to sea before and maimed me. Unlike Ahab, I wanted nothing to do with my old enemy ever again.

It was late when I got home that night. I'm not sure what time it was exactly, but everyone else was asleep. I walked through the front door of my mom's apartment, down a long hall, and up the spiral staircase that led to the loft I called my bedroom. I slipped of my clothes, hung up my coat, and grabbed an old Nirvana shirt from my dresser. I put the shirt on, slid back the soft blue satin covers, and went to bed.

October 3, 2009

I awoke to my phone's alarm, Bach's "Toccata and Fugue in D Minor." This was a nice change from the usual sound of dishes clanking together in the kitchen sink, coupled with thick frankincense smoke filling the apartment. I figured Kate must be sleeping in if she wasn't up cleaning and blessing the house like it was an ancient temple. She usually got up early to cleanse the apartment both physically and spiritually with her little ritual. When she wasn't busy cleaning, she was yelling at me for not doing so. One of her few rules was that the house had to be immaculate.

If you were asked to wash the dishes, in my household it was implied that you were also to wipe the counters down with bleach, sweep and mop the kitchen floor, and take out any trash. Kate would throw a fit if I had the audacity to do the dishes alone, without completing the other tasks. All West Indian children are taught about cleanliness in this way. Kate grew up with a housekeeper, but she was still expected to clean her own room. Parker was supposed to assist me with these duties, but he pretended to be so incompetent that his help was more of a liability.

I rolled out of bed, grabbed my phone and read my texts messages. There were a few party invites, jokes from friends, but the most eye-catching was a text from Alessandra. The ever-alluring Alessandra. I had agreed to meet with her and a couple of her friends today. I walked into my bathroom, performed the usual early morning rituals and walked out now dressed in shorts and a Sex Pistols shirt I had cut the sleeves off. I grabbed a water bottle and my mp3 player from the nightstand, put on Neutral Milk Hotel and stretched a bit for a few minutes before walking back down the stairs. I then walked through the hall to the other side of the apartment and knocked on my little brother's bedroom door.

"Parker I'm going for a run."

"Ok Col," he replied while he strummed his acoustic guitar. I left the apartment. I reached the stone floored lobby of our black and white apartment complex through big glass double doors and headed out towards the sidewalk. The palm trees outside swayed with the slight autumn breeze. I went for a run like I had every Saturday morning. I ran down the block passed neighboring buildings. I passed some children playing and a middle-aged woman walking her Yorkshire terrier. I continued down White Oak Avenue and up towards Rose Lawn, the nearby cemetery. I ran by the brick walls that lined the elaborate burial grounds and passed the great, black, iron-wrought gate that welcomed mourners. As I passed the cometary, I reflected on everything that had happened in the last year.

I thought about Alessandra and the moral implications of our little affair. I thought about Lexie and the nice afternoon we'd spent together. Suddenly, without a warning, *she* crept into my thoughts. I ran faster and harder to try to drown her out of my mind. I ran that way until I reached Hillcrest Street, two miles away. I was too tired to think about anything but rest, so I stopped and drank some water. I took a few deep breaths, then prepared for the run back home.

By the time I reached home there was a note on the smooth granite bar that protruded from the kitchen counter. It read "gone to run errands, love Mom." I tossed the note in the waste bin and headed back up to my room to shower. After about thirty minutes I rose feeling refreshed. I put on fresh clothes and walked over to the bed where my cell phone lie. I had a missed call. I checked the log, saw an unfamiliar number, and decided to call it back.

"Hello," said the person on the other end.

"Hi, my name's Colin Prescott, you called me?"

"I was hoping you still had the same number bro."

"Tyson?" I said, instantly recognizing the voice.

"Yeah, how have you been?" Tyson said. Tyson Montes was the closest thing to a best friend that I'd allowed myself to have since the incident. You know, the incident where my high school best friend and I had a brutal falling out. It was so juvenile looking back. Of course, it was over a girl. I've always thought it was futile to prioritize relationships over friendships at our age. I mean who do you have to turn to when the relationship ends? It's insane how build a friendship with someone for years and abandon that forged bond over a person we only just met.

If I'm being honest, I can't say I was really all that into her. I just liked the attention. It would have all been fair and well, if it were just a competition. He won. I lost. It could have been that simple, but that wasn't how things played out. I'd confided in him that she hit on me after a party one night. I admitted that I had a bit of a crush on her but wasn't sure if it was fair to make a move. The situation was convoluted as it wasn't just the two of us involved. A third friend of ours harbored feelings for her too. I ultimately decided to exit this little love quadrangle because of that. I wasn't interested in fighting over a girl.

She was kind of a recluse, which didn't mesh well with my lifestyle anyway. There were plenty of fish in the sea. My so-called best friend and I talked about this in depth. He placated me with some bullshit about how our third friend wasn't really a factor. He played to my ego masterfully. The whole time he was just listening and keeping his little secret. I'm not sure what possessed him to finally tell the truth, but I was so vexed I had to physically leave campus after he did. I hadn't been that mad since the sixth grade, when I blacked out and broke a bully's nose for picking on my brother.

Naturally, the incident led to distance. It also led to a brief fistfight outside of a movie theater in Burbank. He landed a single punch. I was wearing some cheap shoes at the time, and one slipped off as I got thrown off balance. Our friend group promptly stepped in and split us before it could escalate any further. I was seething. He was about 110lbs heavier than me, but I didn't care. As we drove off, our friends had to actively keep me from exiting the car to catch up with him on foot.

My blood was boiling. I could feel white hot rage simmering beneath my skin. I also heard Kate's voice in my head reminding me to control myself. I wasn't in the sixth grade anymore. The scales were not equal. I couldn't allow myself to be the angry black man in public. I couldn't let anyone enrage me to the point of no return. I'd end up in jail or worse.

He apologized profusely less than 24 hours later, all while he was gossiping about his victory. Pathetic. We were like brothers in my eyes until then. I've come to realize that my vision was heavily distorted. We were never really even friends. He was always an adversary in disguise. He was always a two-faced coward. I just didn't see it until the wool had been removed from my eyes. This last betrayal was in addition to many other little slights.

I had heard all the rumors he spread about me at VVHS. I knew all about how he tried to sleep with my ex, and how in my absence he made jokes at my expense. He was usually trying to one up me, desperately trying to even the playing field, but that was all back in high school. I chalked it up to insecurity and friendly competition. I assumed that once we graduated, we had crossed the threshold into reality. We were young adults. Things were going to be different, or so I thought.

When I first heard that he was talking about our little scuffle, I wanted to put on some good tennis shoes and invite him to meet me at the nearest park so we could finish it. I wasn't going to be satisfied until one of us had drawn blood. I seethed about it for weeks. I thought about confronting him at school or in front of his parent's house. My thirst for revenge grew by the hour, but the bigger part of me knew it wasn't worth it. Any joy I'd get from exacting revenge would be fleeting. It wasn't going to dissolve the feelings of bitterness and embarrassment that flooded me. I decided the healthiest thing to do was to let it go.

I severed all our ties, which was easier than I thought. He quickly faded from the social scene due to his penchant for deceit and generally acerbic personality. I learned rather quickly that most of our shared friends only really tolerated him for my sake. Last I heard he'd started hanging with some washed up coke heads from Reseda. Anyhow, Tyson was the closest thing I'd had to a best friend since all that drama went down. He was one of the few people I trusted before he went away to Pepperdine last year. We haven't spoken all that much since then. Tyson was adjusting to university life and my life was the same level of hectic it had always been.

"I've been alright, how about you?" I asked.

"This school is too religious for my taste," he said.

"I found it odd that *you* had found Jesus."

"The only thing I found was a scholarship."

"Ah that explains it." We chatted for a good fifteen minutes. We truly missed each other's company. We recounted some of our wild exploits, the way old friends do. We once shoplifted on a dare from a certain overpriced, preppy, retailer together. We took magic mushrooms for the first time together. We'd almost been arrested once together.

There were so many cherished misadventures all our friends knew about but were fiercely guarded from our parents. He was driving down from Pepperdine later, so we agreed to meet at around 9:00 pm. When Tyson and I go out together it's an awesome and cataclysmic event. Awesome to observe, cataclysmic for those we left in our wake. Tyson is strikingly handsome. He's tall, athletic, with dark hair, grey eyes, and a sense of humor that can complement any situation.

We share a love of The Clash, The Smiths, and Joy Division. Combined we were nearly irresistible, or at least it felt that way. We made the city our hunting ground. We prowled through parties, rooftop mixers, and nightclubs looking for single girls. We waded into vacant rooms, closets, and any other secluded spot we could find, ready to eagerly devour each one. It was always the same. These girls knew the game, but no matter how smart, beautiful, or resolute, they found themselves entangled with us.

Don't get me wrong, the adoration was addictive. The problem was that neither I, nor Tyson, returned the sentiment. We tried to be respectful about it. We tried to avoid being cold, but sometimes these things can't be helped. An air of detachment can be wildly attractive anyway. I grew excited as the hours passed. I ate a light dinner and showered. At 8:25 pm, I gathered my favorite cologne, a black blazer, a light blue button-down shirt, and dark denim jeans. I put the outfit on with the blazer last. By the time I was done, Tyson had called to say he was downstairs.

When I got outside, I found him nursing a cigarette. Tyson was impeccably dressed himself and leaning against the driver's side of his Nissan roadster. He offered me a cigarette and I accepted. I got into the car and lit up, as we sped off into the night. Tyson made sure to roll the windows down and blast the car fan to prevent any second-hand smoke from clinging to the interior of the vehicle. We reached downtown within minutes. Downtown Villa Valle was magnificent at that hour. Lights gleamed across the sky from towers holding offices and hotel rooms. Cars zoomed past one another, while bits and pieces of songs emanated from them and hung in the crisp night air. Streams of pedestrians in layered garments flooded the crosswalks and cafés. It was quite a sight to see. "Wake up" by Arcade Fire, blared from the car stereo.

When we reached Cosgrove St, Tyson made a left turn. After a while he parked. I stepped out the car first and onto the pavement. Tyson followed not far behind until we were side by side. We walked down the smooth red brick driveway to the splendid little house where we'd be spending the night. Music blasted out through the open windows. Tyson approached the giant oak door first. He used the ancient looking iron-wrought knocker to announce our presence. A short, cute, girl with blonde hair and bright brown eyes, answered the door. Her name was Josslyn Rowe. She'd always had a crush on Tyson, but not because of his reputation, despite it. Up until before he left for college Tyson had never reciprocated. Before then he had been the popular lacrosse player. She was a band geek and a senior at VVHS.

Tyson described moving away for college as liberating and terrifying. He had never known such crushing loneliness. He had to start over in a new city, at a new school, and make an entirely new set of friends. Making friends meant joining clubs and activities. He was a fairly social guy, but I could see how overwhelming it would be to have to put yourself out there all over again. I was relieved that I stayed in my little cocoon of Villa Valle for a while by going to Villa Community College (not like my grades were competitive enough to go anywhere else).

One moment in July of last year, Tyson ran into Josslyn at a party at his school and they wound up sleeping together. After it happened, Tyson began pretending that it hadn't. He hadn't spoken to anyone about it except for me and he swore me to secrecy. Josslyn was attractive, albeit geeky. She was 18, though still a senior at VVHS.

At first, I thought he was just embarrassed that she was still in high school. When I realized that wasn't it, I started to think that maybe he had deeper feelings for her too.

He could have slept with anyone else, but he didn't. He blurted this out to me on the way to her house. There wasn't enough time to discuss it before we arrived. Not enough time to unravel his feelings on the subject. I figured he wanted it that way. I listened to the whole story and told him not to worry about it. I knew Josslyn and she was too much of a WASP to cause a scene at her own party.

"Come on in guys," she said greeting us together.

"Josslyn, how have you been?" I said, as she and I shared a warm hug.

"Good, it's great to see you!" she said with her usual bit of enthusiasm.

"It's been too long Joss," Tyson added hugging her. Tighter than I had.

"Definitely, I'm glad you came." We waded through the crowd to the kitchen island that held alcohol and several shot glasses. I felt a little thrill. I walked up to the counter, grabbed a clean glass and filled it with rum. I slid it to Tyson, then filled two more for me and Josslyn.

"To friendship," I said. We all clinked shot glasses and downed our rum. We repeated this ritual twice more. Each time one of us gave a different toast. Tyson's toast was to youth. Josslyn's toast was to a hell of a night. The second and third shots felt warm and comforting going down. I downed a beer in quick succession to ensure I had a good buzz going, then left the kitchen. I tapped Tyson on the shoulder on my way out to let him know. I moved out towards the living room which had become a giant dance floor, and a graceful brunette grabbed my hand.

It was Alessandra. She was decked out in Egyptian style earrings, a matching necklace, and a short yet not too revealing white dress. She looked glorious. The skin she let show gleamed, even underneath the dim light. We danced to song after song. Sometimes she would pull me in close then push me away again just to add a little spice to things. Meanwhile, Tyson was off with Josslyn somewhere, no doubt. I had noticed the way they looked at each other at her front door.

Knowing this meant I didn't have to try so hard to mingle and that I didn't try to hook-up with a new girl, if I didn't want to. I didn't want to at that moment. All I wanted to do was continue to be lost in the music with Alessandra. But of course, we eventually grew tired. She suggested we rehydrate, and I obliged. As we walked hand in hand back towards the kitchen, I noticed a couple making out in the corner of the room. They kissed and groped at each other wildly. They were haff-reclined on a loveseat. The guy was facing toward us. The girl's face was obscured from view. Their passion intensified with the music.

The guy kissed her neck, all the way down her chest to her cleavage. At that moment, I got a better look at the girl. My blood ran cold when I saw her face. My thoughts ceased to concentrate on anything except for her. I couldn't hear the music anymore, or even feel Alessandra's hand, which tightly gripped mine. I couldn't feel anything. Shoulders brushed past me and the tiled floor felt like putty beneath my feet. All I could see was her. Leona Cavanaugh was 5'6", with soft brown eyes, and curly black hair. She had glistening dark skin and an exceptionally curvaceous figure. She was one of the most beautiful girls I had ever known.

All I could think about was her face locked in that familiar look of ecstasy, as this random guy kissed her everywhere that had once been sacred to me. The girl was Leona Cavanaugh of course and I was devastated at the very sight of her. I knew I had to keep moving. The party wasn't going to end because Leona was in the corner of a room getting hot and heavy with some guy. Alessandra still wanted water after all. She grabbed a bottle off the counter and drank some, I grabbed the vodka once more and poured it into the first glass I found.

"You sure that's good for exhaustion?" Alessandra asked cautiously.

"Who's exhausted?" I said with a smile. I took a shot for each swig of water she took. I was up to eight, before I took her hand again. I led her past where Leona was seated. As we reached the loveseat, I kissed Alessandra, slow and tender right in front of Leona and her mystery guy. We resumed walking until we floundered into one of the spare bedrooms in the Rowe family's house. I closed the door, and she locked it. I wrapped my arms around her waist. I kissed her again, this time more passionately than I had outside. She matched my intensity.

We waltzed over to the bed just across the room. We swayed over it, kissing. She pushed me down onto it and kissed me rough. We locked lips for several minutes. I rolled her over and hovered above her. I kissed her hard and sweet. I kissed down the left side of her neck, all the way to her breasts. I went in for a kiss on the lips and she bit neck. It was unexpected and tantalizing. She took off my blazer and unbuttoned my shirt. I hiked up her white dress. The alcohol shouted, *go for it. Colin, go for it!* I started to, but then she stopped me.

"I'm not ready," Alessandra said. She placed her hand on top of mine, where it lay on her thigh. I fell on the bed beside her. "Are you upset with me? I'm sorry."

"No. I would never want you to do anything you aren't ready for."

"Are you sure? I didn't mean to get you started and then just stop."

"No, really, it's alright. It just makes you more fascinating," I said. Then I kissed those raspberry lips of hers, wrapped my arms around her shoulder and let her lay her head on my chest. We slept there for an hour or so, before we heard a knock on the door. We fixed ourselves up. I buttoned back my shirt. She pulled down her dress, tousled her hair, and opened the door shamelessly.

We discovered Tyson on the other side. He was ready to go. I grabbed my blazer and walked out of the room. Alessandra followed. I kissed her goodbye, and she melted back into the crowd. Tyson and I said goodbye to Josslyn. When he thought I wasn't looking Tyler slipped her a kiss on the cheek. We walked out and to the car. We were silent until we drove back down Cosgrove St towards downtown. It was a tense silence, the kind that filled the air and buried everything in it. It must have become unbearable for him, because Tyson broke it. He asked me if everything was okay.

"Yeah, why do you ask?" I said trying to seem aloof.

Tyson read right through it. "You've been quiet ever since we left Josslyn's."

"I'm fine," I said trying to brush it off.

"Are we friends or what?" he asked matter-of-factly.

I stared out the window for a moment. I almost couldn't form the words and then they spilled out with reckless abandon. "I saw Leona going at it with some kid."

"Wow," Tyson said stunned. He placed a hand on my shoulder in a show of support. I took a deep breath. "Wanna go get stoned and order pizza?"

"I thought you'd never ask," I said. It was nice not to have to get into the specifics. He just understood. It was no secret how I felt about Leona. Anyone who was around us for more than a minute could see it. I acted like a hopeless puppy dog around her. Tyson and I laughed then lit more cigarettes.

"What happened with you and Joss by the way?" I asked.

"Nothing worth talking about," Tyson said.

"I know what you're doing, and I appreciate it, but I'm ok. I swear. I can tell that something happened between the two of you. Tell me all about it."

Tyson told me everything that happened after that. When we reached his house, he took a deep breath. I assured him it would all work out in time. I couldn't think of anything else to say. We spent the rest of the night eating slices of double-cheese pizza and watching the *Count of Monte Cristo*. When I woke up the next morning I was sleeping on Tyson's bed and Tyson had created a makeshift bed on the floor out of an open sleeping bag and several pillows. I gathered my things and started for the front door, so that I could head home. Tyson would have gladly given me a ride, but it had been a long night, and I didn't want to wake him. He had done enough for me already by just being there and listening.

When I arrived back home, the first thing I did was check the parking garage to see if Kate's car was still there. My mom always woke up early on Sundays, not to attend any sort of religious service but to run errands and lunch with her girlfriends. When I looked, I noticed her black Chevy trailblazer was absent from the designated space. This afforded me plenty of time to clean myself up and relax without having to answer a barrage of questions. I strolled in as I had done two nights before, showered, changed, and slept for a bit.

When I got up again it was 1:00 pm. I made myself an egg sandwich and cleaned up my mess. Tyson called to see if I wanted to play tennis. It had been our Sunday morning ritual before he left for Pepperdine, so of course I said yes. We were lousy at it, but it was a fun way to catch up and get exercise. He came to pick me up about 30 minutes later. I grabbed my favorite black and blue racquet and headed down to meet him. He drove us to Emerson Park, which had the best tennis courts in town. Tyson parked his roadster in the main structure behind the park. We retrieved our racquets and walked across the damp green field that separated the lot from the park. We stepped onto the clay floor the first empty court we found, and each took our positions at opposite ends of the net.

"You want to serve?" Tyson asked.

"Sure," I said.

I stood behind the baseline threw the little yellow-green ball into the air and whacked it across the net with my racquet. He received it and returned with great veracity. After a few rounds he asked for the full story of what went down with Leona. First and foremost, her family from Anguilla. This mutual connection to the West Indies, made the relationship feel special. It hadn't occurred to me that I hadn't shared all of the details with him, but I was felt extremely guarded. The wound was still fresh. I was still healing. "I fell for her, and everything went to hell.

There isn't much more to say than that," I said trying desperately to sound cool and casual. Tyson must have read the way I said it. He could tell that wasn't the entire story, but it was all I was ready to share at that moment.

He knew me well enough to know that if he dropped the subject for now, he'd probably get the rest of what happened out of me later. So, he dropped the subject and offered empathy instead. I was grateful. The whole truth was much more painful than I was willing to admit.

The whole truth was, Leona and I spent almost every waking day with each other, all of spring and well into the summer. By August I hadn't just fallen for her, I had fallen completely in love with her. I loved the way she smelled. I loved the way she laughed, and that mischievous smile of hers. I loved how she would dance to salsa across her living room floor, when we were alone. I even loved when she was mad, how habitually clean she was. I loved everything about her. We would have made the perfect couple, but bad timing and immaturity stood in our way.

For one, when I met her, I was diligently pursuing her best friend, Ivy. Ivy was pretty and slender, with green eyes, but wasn't nearly as stimulating as Leona. I quickly came to detest how she often stared blankly, while me and others discussed politics. She had nothing to add. Any topic except anime was beyond her. That alone eventually ended this pursuit. Not that there's anything wrong with loving anime. I just prefer someone with more than one narrow interest.

By the time I realized it was Leona and not Ivy that I wanted, it was too late. Leona had already become involved in a strictly sexual relationship with a third baseman at our school, Villa Community College. This baseball player seemed like a nice enough guy, but I couldn't stand him. My jealousy raged on in secret as Leona would go into graphic detail about their escapes in her talks with me. Despite this I was still enamored with her. I assumed it was unrequited.

I would later learn she was actively trying to make me jealous. She wanted to get a rise out of me. She wanted to really see if I wanted her back, beyond all the hints and near misses. I was ignorant to that, so I distracted myself the best I could. Sometimes, I buried myself in my studies. Sometimes, I distracted myself with other girls. Unfortunately for me, Leona took it as a sign that my interest in her was shallow. Though she had not been dishonest when she told me she was afraid to lose her freedom, I think she was more afraid to love someone so completely, who wouldn't love her back.

She was determined not to be that weak. Oddly enough it was that same determination that stopped me from confessing my true feelings from the start. Irony and bad timing, but I digress. Tyson and I finished up our match. Tyson won. We headed to Tyson's house to devise a plan for the night. I may have had school the next morning, but that wasn't going to stop me from going out that night. I made a short trip home and met Tyson back at his place an hour or so later.

We drove down Hollywood Boulevard to a place called The Ruby. The Ruby was a swanky little nightclub nestled between a café and the Roosevelt Hotel. I've become somewhat of a regular on the Hollywood club scene as of late. I've come to patronize a few different spots with 18 and over nights – like My Studio, Les Deux, and The Roxy. Unlike those other venues, The Ruby was known for its glorious three-room layout, as well the sexy attendees. Tyson parked at an underground structure just up the street from the club. Since we weren't yet 21 but wanted to drink, we'd secured a bottle of vodka from a local liquor store. In the suburbia, there's always a store clerk that will sell you booze, as long as no one finds out. We commenced taking shots before we got out of the car. We took three shots each just to get ourselves started. We then poured as much as it took to fill Tyson's medium-sized flask, which he then hid in the waistband of his underwear.

We both knew he didn't have to do much more to conceal it as this club's security focused mainly on the age limit. The line moved swiftly and after a quick pat down we were in. Like two heartless fiends we separated and spread out into the crowd in the first room, the largest room searching for "picks." Tyson spotted his pick right away, a busty, doe-eyed brunette. I moved in deeper amid the sea of writhing bodies then I set eyes on my pick. She had a silky-smooth silhouette, when I approached further, I could see her full frame. She danced with her arms high above her head, fingers caressing her wrist and forearm in a seductive manner.

She was carefree and captivating. I moved towards the girl, closer, and closer until I was at her side. She turned towards me and then looked away. She was dressed in a tight cream shirt, black miniskirt, and cream pumps. She whirled her hair around teasingly. I danced directly in front of her, so I could look into her eyes for the first time. They were the same shade of caramel as her hair. They seemed full of ambition and innocence.

"What's your name?" I asked my voice soft and smooth on purpose.

"Huh?" she said, trying to hear me over the music. I'd forgotten where we were for a moment. I scooted in closer to her and attempted the introduction again.

"What's your name?" I shouted this time. I watched her eyes light up in a way that signaled that she finally telegraphed what I had said.

"Kelly," she said with a smile. She had perfect, pearly, white teeth.

I took a turn at introducing myself. I kept the same volume I had when I asked her name for the second time. "I'm Col..."

"Colin Prescott," she interrupted. "I know." I was genuinely surprised. This had never happened to me before. I'd occasionally run into someone, who recognized me from school or a party, but that was always in town. We were well outside of Villa Valle city limits. It was kind of cool. "How?" I uttered.

"I go to Villa Valle High School," she said confidently.

"Oh, so you're a senior at VVHS?" I asked cautiously.

"Sure," she said dancing around wildly. I knew she wasn't by that response.

"How old are you?" I should have known she was underage because she didn't answer right away. After some back and forth, she confessed that she used her sister's ID to get in. She was a junior and had just turned 17. She was only a few years younger than I was, but I wasn't too sure about it. Dealing with a high school girl post-graduation was the kind of thing I'd always judged other guys harshly for. It was picking low-hanging fruit. I didn't want to be that kind of guy, but I also didn't want to be the kind of sap I was before with Leona or my ex-best friend. I was determined to reinvent myself, so I indulged her.

"Promise you won't tell the bouncer?" She said flirting. She must have telegraphed my hesitance, because she immediately pivoted to asking how old I was. We could hardly hear each other over the music. Trying to talk to someone in a nightclub is the worst. She decided to step in closer to me to remedy that.

"I thought you knew everything about me?" I shouted. She moved in closer.

"A name and a precarious reputation aren't everything," she said.

"I just turned 19 this summer."

"Cool. I love older guys." She winked after she said it. Part of me hated that I enjoyed the attention, but part of me reveled in it. Besides, we were just dancing, and she was a very good dancer. We eventually made our way onto the main stage. The DJ lingered high above us in an enclosed booth. "Close to Me" by The Cure came on. The sound pulsated out of the DJ's booth and through all the speakers. The rhythm and Robert Smith's cool voice filled my body limb by limb. I've always loved The Cure.

I danced towards and away from her, snapping my fingers in unison with the beat. A rousing enthusiasm filled the air. We slid across the stage, which was slick with perspiration and half-spilled drinks. Kelly slid into me. I wrapped my left arm around her waist, and we kissed. As soon as my lips met hers, we drifted away from everything, the music, the stage, the club itself. I stopped the kiss, remembering how old she was. There was only a two-year age difference between us, but it nagged me still.

"I'm going to have a quick smoke and then we can go back on the floor again, sound cool?" I said. I was dripping with sweat and desperately in need of fresh air.

"Of course," she said. Her voice was brimming with excitement. It was the kind of zest for everything in life that only accompanies naïveté. I took her hand and walked out the two giant sliding glass doors that led to the smoker's patio. I grabbed a pack of Marlboro lights from my pocket and the little black lighter that sat next to it. I pulled a cigarette out, placed it in my mouth, and lit it. Kelly stood at my side staring starry-eyed at me.

"Hey, can I have one?" she said. I debated whether to comply or not. She was only 17. Then again, I had been much younger when I had my first cigarette.

"Screw it, why not," I said as I handed her one. She gave her best impression of a sultry, smoldering, stare as she placed the cigarette between her lips. I lit it for her and watched as she took a deep long drag. She coughed feverishly on the exhale, a tale-tell sign that she had never had a cigarette before. She was pulling out all the stops to impress me. I found it kind of cute.

"Ready to dance some more?" I said, putting her out of the obvious misery she was in, having to endure the cigarette. She replied with an enthusiastic yes. We made our way from the patio to the dance floor in the second room. We danced to synthesized pop and electronic remixes of popular rock songs. After a while Tyson came into the room. I told Kelly to wait for a second and walked over to check up on him.

"Are you ready to call it a night, or am I interrupting?" Tyson said.

I checked my phone. It was 1:30 am. The club would be closing in half an hour anyway, so it was a good time to go. "I'm ready when you are. I'll just say goodbye."

"Cool," Tyson replied. I walked back over to Kelly announced I had to leave. She gave me a big hug and a kiss on the cheek. As I turned to leave, she playfully snatched my phone out of my hand and punched her number into the keypad.

"I won't forget tonight," she said in my ear as she saved her number. I simply smiled. On the walk back to Tyson's car he and I exchanged a few words. The night had turned out great for both of us. Tyson told me how the buxom brunette had given him her number on a napkin. She tried to be mysterious and sexy by writing just the letter "A" underneath it, but this posed a problem because he could not recall decisively whether her name was Amber or Ashley. I laughed and told Tyson all about Kelly. When I got to the part about her only being 17, he looked me straight in the eyes and laughed.

"Who the hell cares man?" he said. "There's only a two-year age difference."

"I don't know," I said. "It just feels weird."

"You've been with older women. How is this any different?"

"Hooking up with a senior as a sophomore doesn't count."

"It was still a score."

"Maybe." The wind rushed in through the open car windows, as we drove back down Hollywood Boulevard. The city was ablaze with lights. Big bright taxis sped past us on either side. I was deep in thought about how I'd never date Kelly. I couldn't. Her kisses were too endowed with innocence, but the night had served its purpose. It was the reawakening I needed. The reawakening I missed that night where Alessandra and I almost consummated our relationship at that party.

Classes flew by the following week. Monday and Wednesday, I had

Anthropology and Comparative Philosophy. Tuesday and Thursday, I sat through Art History and Modern Psychology. Friday is my day off. I made sure not to any classes today. I needed a break from endless essays and lectures. Besides, I got a call from Alessandra. If I had scheduled classes, I would have missed it. I smiled at the sound of her sultry voice. She invited me out for a group hang tonight. All of our little jaunts were essentially group hangs. It was the only way Alessandra could convince her conservative family to let her leave the house.

They believed that she would remain chaste, so long as she was surrounded by good influences. They only allowed her to go out if her younger brother agreed to accompany her, or if she was under the watchful eye of a family-sanctioned friend. Since her brother was usually busy with his own social life, the obligation of protecting Alessandra's perceived purity often fell to her pal, Tiffany. Alessandra and Tiffany had known each other since catechism. Like Alessandra, Tiffany was reserved and academically gifted. In fact, Tiffany had been president of the student government at Sacred Heart. Most importantly, her family was extremely pious.

For these reasons, Alessandra's parents trusted Tiffany to a fault. Little did they know, she smoked, drank, and was highly sexually active with her secret boyfriend. I sent a text inviting Will to come along and he agreed. I went to take his shower. After I had dressed, I spritzed my neck with Obsession by Calvin Klein and left for school. Everything after my contemporary music class was a blur. It was one dull lecture by a white-haired, white men after another.

All I could think about was Alessandra. When we finally came face to face, I was not disappointed. As I walked up, I saw her, seated patient and poised on a thin metal chair. She was next to a little glass table outside of Edo Bistro, my favorite Japanese Restaurant. Her friend Tiffany and Tiffany's boyfriend Evan surrounded her. I sat down and we all exchanged hellos. As we mingled, two more people approached us. Dressed in a bohemian flare and moving towards us in vibrant color were Leo Santos and Ezra Wolfe, two of the biggest stoners I had ever met.

Leo's hair was tussled in its normal fashion and Ezra had big gold-rimmed aviator sunglasses covering his eyes. Despite their unparalleled love for cannabis, these guys were also two of my closest and oldest friends. We'd known each other for years. I knew I could trust them. Besides I enjoyed smoking out with them every now and then.

"Colin, can we steal you for a minute," Leo asked.

"Sure," I replied, not knowing what they had in mind.

Once they had walked a safe distance from the table, Ezra started in. "We're going to buy some acid, you want in?" he said.

"How much?" I said without hesitation. In hindsight I really should have considered this more, but I was unraveling. In my head, there wasn't time to ruminate on my choices. I was dedicated to living purely in the moment.

"We'd just need ten bucks from you," Leo answered. I reached into his back left pocket, pulled out my wallet, and handed Ezra five dollars in single bills.

"We'll be right back. Are you still going to be here?" Leo asked.

"I'm waiting for Will to show up so yeah," I replied.

"We'll make it quick," Ezra added. My only experimentation with psychedelics up until that point had been with mushrooms before. The hardest drug I tried before was Xanax and that was during senior year at VVHS on a whim. Acid was different. Sure, I'd always been open-minded, but I guess I just hadn't had the opportunity. I was perfect for this kind of experience because I always had a natural disregard for consequences and an unnatural love for adventure. Leo and Ezra returned about ten minutes later and urged me to follow them.

I graciously excused myself from the table with a promise to return and a kiss on Alessandra's hand. We crossed the street and entered an alleyway behind a Lutheran church. Ezra pulled out three little tabs of paper. He placed one under his tongue and handed the others to Leo and me. We both followed suit. Nervousness and excitement seemed to fill the air around us. Only after the little tab dissolved in my mouth, did I think to start asking questions. It was asinine I know, but I asked everything I could think of while still sober.

They assuaged my concerns. They had done it one other time. It was like any other high only more intense. Leo warned me that my heartbeat would increase as I peaked. They said I wouldn't instantly become addicted. They tried it months ago for the first time and hadn't done it since.

They haven't been craving all manner of drugs either. The opportunity had just presented itself and they wanted to try it with me. It all sounded logical. I was in too deep anyway. Ezra pulled out his weed pipe, took a hit, and passed a bowl around. By the time it was my turn to smoke, the LSD started to hit me. I felt my heart racing just as Leo said it would.

I took a deep breath and everything around me became wavy. I wasn't seeing dragons or other mythical creatures, but the color of everything around me seemed much more saturated. Occasionally, I'd look over at a nearby a car or street sign and notice the colors were bleeding from it. It was kind of like painting with watercolors. My body felt weightless. It was like floating on air. It's cliché I know, but there's no other way I can describe it. I took in more of the night air and floated gently across the alleyway back toward Tokyo Bistro.

When I got back to the table I tried to seem as normal as possible. Will had just joined us. We chatted for a few before Alessandra gave me the signal to make an excuse to leave the table. She waited for a few minutes, then excused herself as well. We'd coordinated this beforehand. I don't even remember what my excuse was, all I remember is that the next thing I knew were across the street at the Valle Vista Library. We walked around the back of the library, soon after I had her pressed up against one of the exterior walls of it. Overlooking an empty parking lot, we kissed hot and smooth.

"So, who was that girl?" she asked breathy. Unbeknownst to Alessandra, I had started tripping pretty hard by then. I was desperate to stay in the moment. She was backlit by the glow of the nearby streetlights. She was gorgeous as usual. I kissed down the side of her neck and around her clavicle. I was hoping to avoid the conversation, but she cleared her throat as if to say that she knew I had heard her.

"What girl?" I said finally, in between kisses.

"The one at the party the other night," she said.

"There were quite a few girls at that party?" I said. I continued kissing her neck and hoping my attempts at deflection would succeed.

"You know which one I'm referring to," she said. I furrowed by brow to feign confusion, but she dove in straight for the kill. "The one you were staring at for a bit. The girl in the corner on the loveseat with that boy." She was not going to allow me to distract her. I resented her and admired her for it. I ran my hands down the small of her back. She shivered with excitement. I was making the moves, but she was in control. I knew this was all happening at her will and could stop at her will at any moment. I really didn't want to talk about Leona, but she Alessandra was backing me into a corner so to speak.

"No one important," I said. I figured if I had no choice but to answer, I would keep my answers short. The less details I gave the better.

"Oh, come on, you were staring at her pretty hard. In fact, if I hadn't been pulling you along, I think you would have frozen dead in your tracks."

"I'm glad you were pulling me along then." My hand met hers. I lifted it with her arm above her head and held it there against the cold brick as our lips met again. She started at me intently. I knew she wasn't going to drop the subject. "I don't ask you about the other guys in your life," I added. I could tell she was agitated by this.

"There's only one and I've already told you about him," she said strained. She was trying not to sound flustered. Our situation was rooted in intense attraction and lack of commitment. If either of those elements fell out of balance, we could quite possibly implode.

"Right and I don't make trouble for you about it. You're in love with him, or so you say, and yet here you are with me." I wanted her to hear how ludicrous our situation sounded. It made no sense out loud. We were supposed to be strictly physical.

"I do love him, but distance does things," she reasoned. It was a hollow rationale. Sure, it was human, understandable, but hollow, nonetheless. I kissed further and her further down her neckline. I gently grasped the hand I had pressed against the wall and slide it inside of my pants.

"Oh my!" she said. She unbuttoned my jeans and fondled the outside of my boxer-briefs. She was aggressive, almost feral in her movements and I loved it.

"Feel the guilt dying off?" I said.

"I feel something alright," she said. Her hand teased me further. My eyes nearly rolled back in my head at her touch. She took a couple fingers and pranced them across the waistband of my boxer-briefs. She lowered her fingers slowly grasping my package. I'm no virgin, but I actually gasped out loud when she made contact. We continued kissing and biting each other occasionally. She slowly massaged me from the inside of my underwear. I slid a hand up her skirt and eagerly began to return the favor. We stood there breathing and sighing in delight. The acid pumping through my bloodstream felt like raw electricity. I suppose Alessandra was feeling adventurous, because next she slowly knelt down in front of me. The wind rushed passed us up on the roof of the library. Without missing a second of eye contact, she unbuckled and unzipped my jeans.

What I felt next was sheer warmth and ecstasy. I massaged her shoulders as waves of enjoyment passed through me. We continued until we heard the engine of a car. Someone had come to use one of the library parking spaces. It wasn't legal to park there after hours, but it wasn't uncommon either. I knew this meant the end of our liaison. I wanted to keep going. I wanted to hike up her skirt and return the favor. I probably could have tried to convince her to continue, but I knew she was far too reserved for that. I was surprised and grateful that we had gone this far. We had to get back to our friends anyway. I helped Alessandra to her feet. We were both a bit disheveled and rearranged ourselves. We kissed once more and walked back across the street arm in arm.

"So do I get a name?" she said.

"For whom?" I said. I was tripping so hard that I had forgotten what we were talking about. Alessandra shot me a look that warned me not to keep playing games and the topic of conversation came rushing back to me. "Leona," I confessed.

"Can I get a last name as well?" she said.

"What are you the CIA?" I said. She glared daggers at me. I knew not to push my luck if I planned on ever seeing her again. I very much wanted to continue seeing her. "Cavanaugh," I said. What harm was there in giving her a name. I knew they weren't friends. I knew Leona's friends. At most, they would have known each other in passing in high school.

"What happened with you and this Leona Cavanaugh?" she said. This confirmed she didn't know Leona. I felt instant sigh of relief.

"I loved her desperately. She didn't give a single fuck about me."

"Ah I see. I'm sorry," she said. I had opened up too much. I didn't want sympathy from her. Sympathy isn't sexy. I wanted to remain the object of her desire.

"It's fine," I said trying to save the moment. "It was doomed from the start. Want to go for frozen yogurt?" It wasn't my smoothest transition. She was too smart not to notice, but I was hoping she would give me a pass anyway.

"Sure," she said. I could hear the hesitation in her voice, but she was kind enough to change the subject. We invited a few friends and walked over to The Village. It's Villa Valle's new and only outdoor shopping mall. It's way ritzier than the old mall, with splashes of a few affordable mid-range brands. We found the frozen yogurt shop and ordered quickly. We stayed for a while eating and laughing at little things. After dessert, we all got into Evan's car and took a drive. Tiffany sat in the front next to him. Will sat in the back by one door. Alessandra sat by the other. I sat in the middle between them. It was prime positioning for me to make another move, and I did.

Once we got going, I unfastened his seatbelt, leaned over and starting kissing Alessandra again. I couldn't tell if it was natural attraction propelling me or the LSD I took earlier, but I didn't care either way. I felt like I was covered in sweat, but she didn't seem to notice. All I could think about was her lips on mine. All I wanted was her skin against my skin. She seemed so taken with me - my cologne, my devious smile. She was constantly calling me charming and telling me she couldn't resist me. It was fantastic for my ego. So there next to Will, we got as wild as we could without taking our clothes off. Alessandra's parents called her home about half an hour into it.

As she got out of the car, she stopped to tell me she had broken things off with her boyfriend. I needn't feel any guilt over being the 'other guy' anymore. What she didn't know was that guilt, mixed with the sinfulness of the situation made it more exciting to me. Now I no longer felt like the devil she had made me out to be. I did feel bad for her boyfriend though. I felt like I had stolen her, instead of just "borrowing" her the way I had been doing. Yet still, a part of me was elated. If this was all a game, then I was winning. If I was a thief, I had gotten away with the score successfully.

By the time we reached Will's neighborhood, I had drifted away somewhere. I was lost in the high. Once we'd parked, he shook me out of it. I stood up straight and pretended to be all right, in case his parents were still awake.
He opened the large iron gate to the driveway with his remote. We walked up the pathway and in the house through the back door, as we had done countless times before. That night like the two old friends we were, we played a round of pool. We inevitably started talking about you. Will felt the same way I did. Sadness filled the entire room, then regret, and silence. We decided it was best to change the subject. We each took shots of Jack Daniels in your honor. I probably shouldn't have drank on top of the LSD, but I did it for you. I wish you could have been there. We had a hell of a time. Happy birthday.

October 17, 2009

I've been buried under homework and study guides for midterms. It feels like I have so many simultaneous classes and assignments, that I can barely keep track of them all. Don't even get me started on midterms. It's overwhelming. Of course I've been taking mini-vacations, so I don't lose my mind. One of those vacations happened last night. I caught up with Will over wine and hookah. I awoke at his house this morning on the well-crafted, hideaway bed he had set up for me in his room.

I opened my eyes and stretched out my arms. I rolled onto my side and peered out at the room. It was relatively dark (the way Will had always liked it) save for bits and pieces of morning light that peeked through the natural cracks of the curtains. The same antique lamp sat on the big cherry wood dresser next to the mid-sized television screen that had been there since we were in high school. The same writing desk sat beside the dresser, papers askew on its surface. In fact, pretty much everything in Will's room was the same as I could remember it from high school. The floor was the same perfectly polished lightwood, the ceiling a calming ocean blue with white trim on the molding that surrounded it. The only change was the walls, which had been painted a soft teal. Will awoke rumpling his sheets. I looked over at him.

"Rise and shine bitch," I said jokingly.

"Ah good morning slut," Will replied in an equally playful manner.

I hit him with a pillow. "Shall start the day?"

"I'd like to, but my head is killing me," he said. He looked like he'd been hit by a semi-truck. His skin was paler than usual. His eyes were bloodshot and his hair disheveled. I could tell he hadn't slept restfully, even though were both knocked cold after the night before.

"Mine too, but I know the perfect cure," I said. We slowly rose from our respective beds. Will led the way out of his room and down the small stairs into the living room. We entered the living room and sunshine hit us directly for the first time. It came seeping in through the giant sliding doors that led to the deck.

We passed tasteful post-modern style furniture, ivory sculptures, and art-clad walls en route to the kitchen. I went to the fridge and pulled out orange juice, bacon, and eggs.

"You're going to make breakfast?" Will asked. "That's your big remedy?"

"Trust me, it works," I answered. "Orange juice is for the dehydration. Eggs contain cysteine, which counteracts the effect of acetaldehyde. Acetaldehyde is the byproduct of alcohol metabolism primarily responsible for most of the aftereffects of consumption, a.k.a. our hangovers. And bacon will boost the level of amines in our bodies which will clear our heads." I grabbed a frying and began to prepare our meals. After the eggs and bacon were finished, Will handed me four slices of bread. I made two sandwiches for us out of the contents of the pan.

"So, what happened with Alessandra?" he said. "Did you seal the deal?"

"Not exactly," I said. I knew he was eager to find out all the details, since Alessandra had such a reputation for piety. But I felt that because of that reputation I should probably keep things to myself.

"Come on Prescott, give up the goods," he said.

I thought about how Will was one of my closest friends. If I told him, I didn't think he'd tell anyone. "Okay, but you can't say anything to anyone. I'm trusting you," I said. I then paused for dramatic effect. I could practically see the anticipation building. It was written all over his face. "She gave me a hummer behind the public library."

"No fucking way!" he said in utter disbelief. "I thought she had a boyfriend?"

"It's no big deal. She does, but what's that have to do with me?"

"You kill me."

"Anyway, what are you doing for Halloween?"

"I have a date with Veronica. I should be free on the 30th though. Wanna meet here for drinks and hookah?" I agreed and Will suggested we invite Troy Sanz to join us. Troy Sanz has been friends with Will and I since we were all in the ninth grade. We have however succeeded in this endeavor more than a few times. Unfortunately, he's not much of an extrovert. Getting him to come out the house and hang out with us is always a challenge. If it's an intimate gathering like hookah and drinks at Will's for Halloween, the chances that Troy will make it rise exponentially.

When we finished eating, Will's mom walked into the kitchen. Mrs. Perrin is a tall, thin, blonde in her late fifties with a short-cropped haircut that suits her face perfectly. She'd been a striking beauty in her younger years and still was for a woman her age. She'd also led a very fascinating life before marrying Will's dad. She'd dated the likes of John Ritter and Neil Diamond and was friends with Rory Flynn. The latter relationship led to an instance in which, Mrs. Perrin unknowingly found herself in a lesbian bar being asked to dance by Rory's older sister Deirdre.

Mrs. Perrin declined the invitation but described Deidre as the most beautiful woman and the most handsome man she'd ever see all in one. Anyway, Mrs. Perrin fluttered in wearing a flowing white silk robe and matching pajamas. Kind, sweet, motherly vibes practically emanated from her. I often wondered why my own mother couldn't be more like her.

"Good morning boys," she said. Mrs. Perrin grabbed a pitcher of lemonade from the refrigerator and poured herself a glass. "Do you need anything?"

"Good morning mom," Will said. "I'm fine, thanks."

"Good morning Mrs. Perrin," I said. "Nothing for me, thank you." I was raised not to take too much from people. Kate would have killed me if she knew I was eating breakfast there. She would say, *we don't eat from people.* I was expected to politely decline any meals and wait until I left or got home to eat. It's a cultural thing among West Indians. We tend to avoid eat food cooked from anyone's kitchen, unless they're family or close like family. Although my mom wasn't familiar with Will's parents, I considered the Perrins close enough to feel comfortable eating at their house.

Besides their kitchen was always immaculate, which is the crux of our cultural concern anyway. I knew better than to tell Kate that though. Will let out a small laugh as his mother graciously left the kitchen. It always entertained him that we could be so perfectly polite the moment either of his parents were in our presence, or any parents for that matter. It was like we were going undercover. We cleaned up and left the kitchen. I showered in the guest bathroom, shaved, brushed my teeth and headed home after thanking the Perrins for their hospitality. On the walk home I received a text message from a friend of mine named Kasey. Kasey Chang is one of the most well rounded, high school seniors you will ever meet. Like almost everyone else I know, we met in high school where Kasey is a member of the debate team, choir, student body government, and an expert trombone player.

I'm not sure if you met him, but Kasey is also one of the few publicly gay students in the entire school. You know there's nothing I genuinely appreciate more than being different. So of course, we struck up a friendship and it means a lot to the both of us, I think. Anyhow, Kasey's text read "busy for Halloween?" I replied that I wasn't and asked if he had any ideas and from there the beginning of what would be utter chaos ensued. Kasey and his friends were planning a horror movie night of their own that he was going to host. There would be candy, music, and alcohol. I'm more than thrilled to go, even though they're all seniors at VVHS. I mean they're only a year younger than me and they know how to have a good time.

October 23, 2009

I met with Alessandra in the afternoon, and we fooled around behind the Holy Family Parish School on Van Wynn St. We were almost caught again, like we were behind the library. Only this time we almost got caught twice. It was still worth it. During she asked me if I was seeing anybody else. I tried to evade the subject. She brought it back up and I told her it shouldn't matter. She mentioned she was interested in seeing Ramsey Wallace.

I had known Ramsey from high school. He was one of the only other few black kids at VVHS. I forget how small and white Villa Valle is sometimes. Anyway, immediately after confessing her attraction to Ramsey, she expressed that she didn't think he took her seriously. "He doesn't trust me," she said. "We started talking around the same time you and I began seeing each other."

Apparently, Ramsey was also aware that she had a long-distance boyfriend at the onset of his flirtation with her. She assured me that none of this wouldn't affect us. They were an idea, nothing more. To be honest, I don't really care. Who she sees when she's not with me is none of my business. We're only lovers. I don't expect her to explain anything to me. I met back up with Will at his place this evening and Troy came over. The three of us drank margaritas, smoked hookah, and played music on the rooftop of Will's family's garage. It was chilly, but we danced around so much none of us really noticed. Troy went home around 12:30. I'm sleeping over again tonight.

October 31, 2009

I awoke in the late afternoon. When I got home, Kate had already begun decorating for Halloween. She'd put out pumpkins to welcome trick-or- treaters. The front door and balcony were adorned with fake cobwebs. I showered and prepped myself for another night out, popping an aspirin and drinking down a glass of orange juice to help with my slight hangover in the process. I dressed in a grey t-shirt, flannel button down, and slim dark denim jeans. I drove Kate's sleek black Chevy Trailblazer to Kasey's house. The front lawn was made to look like a cemetery, complete with synthetic fog and faux gravestones. Kasey greeted me at the door and walked me down the long hall to the entertainment room, where his other guests lay sprawled out across the floor and the sofas in the room. I already knew Kasey's closest friends, Adrienne and Chloe.

I was quickly introduced to Adrienne's new boyfriend Owen, Owen's friend, and the friend's girlfriend. I can't quite remember their names, so don't ask me. We watched two different films laughing at the cliché parts and cringing at the gore, until Owen's friend announced he had to take his girlfriend home. We said goodbye to them and the five of us, Adrienne, Chloe, Owen, and Kasey decided to move to Kasey's room. Kasey was reluctant to let us in at first. His excuse was that the room was messy. In reality, I think he was nervous we'd all start hooking up and he'd be left out. Eventually, the girls persuaded him, and he complied. Once we had all walked in, I looked around and made a joke to set him at ease.

"Exactly what mess were you referring?" I said. I gently nudged him in the rib and Kasey let out a little laugh. A look of relief washed over his face and is shoulders relaxed. Adrienne and Owen settled on the floor and started making out, while Chloe and I sat down on Kasey's bed a safe distance from each other. After putting on music, Kasey joined us. We sang along and laughed at each other's random stories. Then we started drinking. We took vodka shots with sprite and cranberry juice chasers. After God knows how many, I changed the music to Sohodolls. I pulled Kasey's office chair out from underneath his desk and started doing a strip routine on it.

I was so glad the chair was wooden and not on wheels. I still have no idea how I came up with a strip routine on the spot, but you know me. I was down to my socks and boxer-briefs in no time.

The next thing I knew Chloe and I started fooling on Kasey's bed. Adrienne and Owen were next to us making out as well. We got pretty hot and heavy, and when Owen left for the bathroom, I stole a kiss from Adrienne. When he got back, we all continued as if nothing happened. Kasey sat there as the four of us rolled around on his bed. The music kept playing and the room seemed to be spinning. I peered over at Kasey for a quick second and noticed a look of great disappointment had settled on his face. It looked as though he was going to cry any moment. It took me a while to realize it, but he hadn't wanted us in his room for this very reason. He knew he'd end up hooking up and leaving him out. He was never concerned with there being a mess. I was just impaired enough to throw caution to the wind.

"Kasey, where's your bathroom?" I asked, breaking my kiss with Chloe.

"You know where it is," Kasey said dryly.

"I forgot. Show me again," I said.

Kasey led me outside of the room and I immediately pinned him up against the wall and kissed him. Maybe it was the alcohol, or maybe it was my way of trying to make up for kissing his two best friends in front of him. All that mattered was that was happening. Kasey was surprised and ecstatic and I was filled with adrenaline.

"Felt like I owed you that," I said smiling,

"You don't owe me anything," said Kasey blissfully. Then Adrienne realized the time. It was about 12:30 am. She announced she had to leave, and I guess Kasey had arranged for his parents to give her and Owen rides home early on. Like a good host, he stood up to go with them.

"You and Chloe can stay here if you like Colin," Kasey said.

"Cool, I'm not ready to go home just yet," I replied.

"Me either," Chloe said. About 15 minutes passed before Kasey returned. During that time Chloe and I spoke some.

I was still undressed, so I decided to put my shirt and pants back on. When Kasey walked back in, he had already come up with an idea for how we'd spend the rest of the night.

"Spin the bottle anyone?"

"I'm up for it," Chloe said.

"I'm in," I replied. There were very few things I can say no to, and this wasn't one of them. Sure, I knew that Kasey was gay, and he had always had a little bit of a crush on me. I also knew there was a very good chance we'd end up having to kiss since there were only three of us, but I didn't care. It was a challenge, and you know I very seldom shy away from challenges. Besides, a kiss is just a kiss. I really didn't think I had anything to lose, and I had already kissed him anyway. Kasey grabbed an empty water bottle. Chloe grabbed a pillow, and I grabbed the bottle of chocolate liqueur Kasey had brought us a little earlier. We passed the liqueur around, each taking a swig as the bottle spun on Kasey's bed.

He had a queen-size bed, with zebra striped covers and pillows everywhere. The bottle landed on Kasey and Chloe first. They gave each other a quick peck and turned back toward me. The bottle landed on them a second time and they kissed for a bit longer, giggling along the way before turning back towards me yet again. The third turn the bottle landed on Chloe and me. We pecked as Chloe and Kasey had. The next turn, the bottle landed on Chloe and me again and we kissed sweetly, but more passionately before turning back towards Kasey.

Then the bottle landed on Kasey and me. We were all a lot more sober by this time and the tension was thick. I cut right through it. Boldly looking into Kasey's eyes, I beckoned him closer. Kasey leaned in, I leaned in, and we kissed ever so lightly. As fate would have it, the bottle landed on us again, after that and the kiss grew a bit stronger, more sensual, more serious. Then we stopped playing the game.

"We're all going to end up hooking up, so who needs the bottle?" Chloe said.

"My thoughts exactly," Kasey said.

He smiled mischievously and that's when I had a sudden attack of conscious.

"That's not going to happen. I may be a bad influence, but I can't corrupt two innocent souls at once," I said. I had been partying since I was 15. I knew neither of them could keep up. It didn't feel right to let things escalate. Besides I hadn't decided how I felt about all of this. Things were moving much faster than I had anticipated.

"Who says we're not already corrupt?" Kasey replied.

"You just want to kiss me again," I said teasingly.

"He got you there Kase," Chloe said.

We all laid back on Kasey's bed and rested. Music flowed through the room, while I stroked both Chloe and Kasey's hair. Every now and then I would catch one of the two just staring at me. It was Kasey more than Chloe. Chloe wanted to remain cool and aloof, but Kasey couldn't help himself. I thought that was very sweet.

At around 3am Chloe's dad called. He was outside of Kasey's house waiting to pick her up. I was surprised how late it was before she had to leave, but Kasey informed me that Chloe's parents are very liberal. When Chloe left and it was just Kasey, and I. Everything was a lot clearer. I was still drunk, but not completely wasted. I fell back onto Kasey's bed and he and I kissed again. Only this time he initiated it and when he went in for another kiss. I didn't resist. Until this day I can't really explain why.

I was never really attracted to Kasey, or any guy, but he was my friend. He was also sweet and not a bad kisser. I had always been open to new experiences, so what if we kissed? I thought to myself at first. I quickly realized I had to stop it. A kiss may have been just a kiss to me, something new and exciting, but it wasn't to him. To Kasey it had potential for something so much more and I couldn't mislead him like that.

"We should stop. I don't want to hurt you," I said. Music blared in the background. Some song I can't recall the words to now.

"Then just keep kissing me," he pleaded. The desperation in his voice was relatable and sad, but it didn't sway me. Rational thought had entered the room, and it wasn't leaving any time soon.

"You know I can't do that," I said.

"Why not?" he said. He had to have known there were a million reasons why that wasn't a good idea. But he sounded earnest, so I explained further.

"Because you're sweet, but this would never go anywhere. I'm not..." I wasn't sure how I was even going to end that sentence, but luckily, he interrupted me.

"You don't have to be, I don't even care. I love you." He was sweet, but jejune. It was ridiculous to believe that he loved me. He hardly knew me.

"No, you don't. Trust me. You are the nicest person I've ever kissed though and one of my favorite people. I feel closer to you now, but I can't keep kissing you just to make you feel better. It will only make you feel worse in the end. And what would it say about me?"

"You're right," he sighed. He sounded defeated, but I knew it wasn't my responsibility to sacrifice my boundaries to make him happy.
I laid back down on Kasey's bed. He laid beside me, and we faded away into the moment. Then there was a knock on the door that got both of us up. It was Mrs. Chang, telling Kasey to turn down the music. I took that as my cue to leave. I rose a bit embarrassed and flashed a smile. I then put my shoes on and told Kasey I should be getting home. It was after two in the morning by then. Kasey walked me to my mom's car. I asked if he had a good time, and he nodded yes emphatically.

"Am I really the nicest person you've ever kissed?" he said.

"Yes. You're the first and only guy too."

"Really?"

"You've made my night."

"See if anyone else said something like that I'd be nauseous, but I really think it's genuine coming from you." I gave him a friendly hug and told him not to worry about what happened. I could tell he wanted to kiss me, but he didn't. As I drove off, I noticed him pause there a little in the rearview mirror, then he walked back into his house. On the way home I couldn't help but laugh thinking about what had just taken place. I had been a crush for my share of girls and now a boy. We kissed and though I couldn't explain it, I did care about him. I couldn't fully understand what had happened beyond that or why it let it happen. But I knew I admired Kasey. He had courage to be himself. He was generous and genuinely kind. I knew firsthand how hard that was to come by in a friend.

November 1, 2009

Kasey and I had a very long talk today. I admitted that it was selfish of me to accept his compliments and lead him on. I guess I just wanted to hear those things and be able to believe that the person saying them really meant it, because I don't think anyone else ever has. He insisted that I deserved to hear them, and he meant them.

"You're a beautiful boy, inside and out. I mean that," he said. When the conversation ended, I wanted nothing more than to believe that. I showered and made breakfast which I ate in my room. Halfway through eating I smiled at the thought that what Kasey said could be true. I enjoyed that someone could really think of me that way, someone who meant it anyhow. When I finished my meal, I made my way back downstairs to place the dish and glass in the sink.

Before I even reached the kitchen, Kate came fluttering down the hallway. She was impeccable even first thing in the morning. She wore a bright red satin robe, with black trim and a golden dragon the peaked around the back and up the left shoulder. Underneath the robe she wore a black gossamer nightdress. Her skin was a smooth, flawless, sea of cocoa. Her hair wavy, glossy, jet-black, laid precise about her shoulders, and her almond shaped eyes looked almost sweet, beneath the sunlight that came in through the windows.

"You do still live here," she said in a lovely yet sharp tone. It was a drain running into her. I much preferred it when we'd just miss each other at home. Two narcissists passing in the night.

"Yep," I said. "Unfortunately," I huffed under my breath.

"I haven't seen you in centuries and all you can say when I do is 'yep?'"

"My apologies, allow me to excuse myself and go improve my diction."

"Better, but not quite the response I was looking for."

"Love you too Mom." I was trying to conclude the conversation, but she wasn't done with me yet. She was primed for a fight. She was going to drag this out as long as she could.

"I'm just wondering what's going on with you. You're out galivanting all over town at all hours of the night. You treat this place like a hotel, and you never speak to me unless you want money."

"That last part's not true," I said. I was being glib by addressing only her last point. I knew it incensed her. "I tried speaking to you several times about non-monetary issues, but then I realized your ability to retain anything that doesn't immediately fascinate you is practically non- existent."

"Oh, hello my name is kettle."

"Ok, well as much as I do love these little chats, gotta run. See you later."

"Don't get arrested and don't get anyone pregnant!"

I sprinted out of the apartment and by the time I returned it was 1:00 am. Unlike all the other times I'd gone out, Kate had stayed up waiting for me. She was menacing, unwelcoming, yet cool. I could tell she intended to argue with me, just by her demeanor. And I was right. She walked over to me and began ranting about how I was never home. It was different than our earlier exchange. It was harsher. She complained that this wasn't the Four Seasons and that I couldn't just come and go as I pleased. That was all par for the course, but it was evident that she had a few glasses of wine and there was an added fire to her voice. She groaned that I needed to start showing a little responsibility.

"I work and go to school, that's not responsible enough for you?" I said tongue laden with vitriol. I couldn't restrain myself. I was sick of her impossible standards. Being from a proud West Indian family, I was expected to be exceptional at every turn. The Eugènes and the Prescotts were both overachievers. My great-grandfathers on both sides, were fortunate enough to own their own businesses and properties, at a time where black families were still struggling to establish economic independence.

"You don't contribute to the household."

"Run out of alimony already huh?

"Don't get smart with me!"

"How much are we talking because I only make minimum wage?"

"I don't know, how much can you contribute?"

I knew telling Kate exactly how much I made would lead down a slippery slope. I watched her take money from my sister, Traci and closely guard the child support and alimony checks she received from my and Parker's dad when we got them. I thought about everything hard for a moment. I didn't have much time to answer because she'd know I was formulating a lie or an excuse, so I just blurted out that I could pay one bill, like the light bill or the gas. Her response was that lights and gas are nothing. It made no sense. She clearly had a bill she already wanted me to pay in mind. I dug deep and asked.

"Pay the internet."

"That would be my whole check in a good week."

"So? You've ignored all of my rules. If you want to be a grown adult so badly, you can pay me like one. I'm tired of my warnings going unheeded. Those who can't hear must feel."

There isn't a phrase I resented more than "those who can't hear, must feel." It was the classic response from a West Indian parent. All I could think about was how unreasonable she was being. How was I supposed to get to school or eat or do anything? She was so money-hungry. She tried to milk me by forcing me into child acting and when that didn't work, she sued dad for child support. Never mind the fact that he's bought all my school supplies and clothes since I was seven. I was disgusted with her. I scoffed and walked past Kate, up the stairs to my bedroom.

November 2, 2009

I awoke early this morning to Kate screeching my name, while hovering over me. She was holding her cell phone. She demanded that I get up, announced that my sister Traci wanted to talk to me, and shoved the phone onto my ear. Then stormed out the room leaving Traci to do her dirty work. No matter the island, traditional West Indian mothers love to call close friends and relatives to talk bad about you. They'll discuss your failings right in front of you too, as if you aren't even in the room. If you're really messing up, they'll implore the relative to talk some sense into you. Kate had regaled her friends, my grandmother, and my great-aunts with tales about my sordid deeds on numerous occasions. The deeds she was aware of anyway. I knew right away that's what was happening here with Traci. I picked up the phone and my sister, attempting neutrality, asked what happened this time.

"I'm not certain. She hasn't been here in weeks and out of nowhere she goes off," I said. I could never predict when she'd be in a mercurial mood.

"Well, she says she's worried about you," Traci said.

"Doesn't one have to be human to worry?" I asked teasingly.

Traci couldn't help but laugh. She swiftly grew serious again. "We both know how she is, but you just have to put up with her for a few more years. Once you can move out on your own, things will get better between you two."

"Why are we even discussing this, you don't like her any more than I do." I wished Traci was more of an ally and a sibling, than a neutral third-party sometimes.

"True, but she is our mother, and we only get one. Just play nice with her."

"I'll try. Do you want to talk to Lucy again?"

"Lucy?"

"It's what I call her sometimes, short for Lucifer."

"Oh Colin! You're lucky she lets you go out. When I was a teen, she would always conveniently dream of calamity right before I would leave the house to go out with friends."

She wasn't joking either. I remember how Kate would stop Traci from leaving the house because she had a dream something bad was going to happen. West Indian mothers are serious about their prophetic dreams. I got out of bed and walked down to the living room in my pajamas. When I noticed my mother wasn't there, I walked down the hall to her bedroom door and knocked. After a minute or two she answered the door, trying to retain her composure.

"Your phone Madame," I said, handing it to her and holding back a smile. She grabbed her phone and slammed her bedroom door. She had been hoping a talk from Traci would have a greater effect on me. She had been using the tactic of gaining sympathy from others and subjecting me to lectures from them for years. I knew this trick the best and unfortunately for Kate, so did Traci. Kate spent several moments in her room after realizing her plan failed. Then in a fury, she rushed out and back up the stairs to my room. I was seated, relaxed, and listening to music when she entered.

"Why don't you respect me?" Kate said.

That's a complex question," I said. I could tell she had had a couple glasses of wine and was seeking out an argument. But I was resolved to be honest. It was complex. I'd felt both smothered and abandoned by her, intermittently over the years. How was I supposed to put all of that into words?

"Sum it up then," she said.

"Well, I find it ridiculous how you have flashes of wanting to be a mother and a stern one at that when you were hardly ever there for me."

"I was there for you!"

"No, you weren't. You were always working, or going to some club meeting, or dating. If it wasn't one thing it was another."

"So what? I like to keep busy."

I knew I had a slim chance of winning this argument from the outset yet filled with foolish pride, I persisted. Part of me wanted to claim victory, but a larger part of me wanted her to see reason. "And you have an excuse for everything."

"I do not. I've been here for you. You just choose not to remember."

"That's not true. I do remember when you used to be there for me. It was early in my childhood when you thought I had the potential to be a star. You paid a copious amount of attention to me then. After I told you I didn't want to act anymore that just dissolved. By middle school the only time you noticed me was when I was getting into trouble. By the time I was in high school I got better at covering things up, so you hardly noticed me at all. That is unless we were having a disagreement. That's pretty much where we stand today. Aside from that I find you hypocritical, unreasonable, irrational, hot tempered, rude, and unfeeling most times."

Kate fell silent. "Well, if you despise me so much and there is so much distance between us, you can get the hell out of my house ASAP."

"Alright," I said. I'd spent many nights struggling to get my points across to her. I had hoped she'd realize the mistakes she'd made with Traci. I had hoped she wouldn't repeat those same mistakes with me and Parker, but here we were.

November 7, 2009

I decided to spend the day inside for a change. I read some, listened to music, watched the clouds float across the pale blue sky, and sipped hot tea to keep warm since the weather cooled a bit. Then I heard a knock on the front door. I rose from the comfortable leather office chair I was seated in. I hadn't invited anyone over, *who could this be?* I descended the stairs carefully and a bit anxious. I walked down the hall and across the living room and then I reached the door. When I opened it, *she* was there. Standing before my very eyes, she was a vision in scarlet and black. Her skin was flawless as usual. Her curly hair hung about her shoulders. Her eyes lit up and fixed upon me. As I approached, her ruby red lips parted, and a smile slid across her face. She was happy to see me, much to my surprise.

"What are you doing here?" I said, trying to speak calmly.

"I'm here to see you, obviously," she said just as calm.

"Well, I wasn't expecting anyone."

I hadn't seen her since early late August, and that was the best I could think of. I wasn't expecting anyone. I hated when my wit failed me. I hate when my mouth went dry, and my mind could only remember the simplest of phrases. But that always happened when she was around and now after everything, it was still no different. I decided I wasn't going to pull any punches. It was speak now or never.

"Why are pretending everything should be okay between us?"

"What would you do in my situation?"

"I'm unsure what situation you're in exactly."

"I miss you. I miss our friendship."

"So now what?"

"Umm, you'll wake up." That's when I awoke in the leather office chair. The End of the Affair by Graham Greene, lay face down on the desk beside me. I had been reading it before I drifted off. My teacup sat next to it. *I knew it was too good to be true.* I stared out at my bed from where I was seated. My mind slipped away from to one particular night this past summer.

It was unbearably hot. I was alone in my room with Leona. I seated on the floor with my back against the bed and Leona sat next to me. We were talking, laughing, and watching television. I couldn't remember what show was on or why she had come over, but none of that was important to this memory. We were there with our backs up against the bed, mocking little things about what we were seeing. Then she moved closer, placed her head on my shoulder, and our conversation grew a bit more serious.

"You know I always wanted to be an actress," she said.

"Really?" I asked. I asked this even though I had known full well she did. She had mentioned it a million times, but I didn't mind hearing it again.

"Yes, and I don't know why, but I always wanted to."

"Well, you're dramatic enough for it," I joked. I always managed to be able joke with her, no matter the topic. It came in handy more than you'd think. I told her she would have made a fantastic actress, that she could still be one if she tried. She said she was determined not to throw herself into the perilous pit of has-beens and hopeless starlets. Then she added that she was too fat to be an actress. I called her delusional.

She raised her head and looked me directly in the eyes, "but I am fat."

"No, you aren't. And even if you were, you'd still be beautiful and perfect."

"Thank you."

She rested her head back on my shoulder and I put his arm around her. We stayed like that for a while, just watching silently. The memory faded out and I returned to reality. There was a knock at the door. I rose. I stopped. I couldn't believe it. I actually pinched myself. *It couldn't be. Am I really awake? What's going on? Only one way to find out.* Just like in my dream I made my way down the spiral stairs and to the door. And when I opened it, I found it was only my younger half-brother Parker. I hadn't even realized he had left. I asked where he had been.

"Went for a bike ride with a friend," he said.

"A girlfriend?" I asked in that mocking tone only teasing siblings use.

"Yes," he said meekly.

"Ok wait. Like a girlfriend, or a friend that's a girl?"

"Friend that's a girl ...for now.".

"Aw how sweet, my little brother is growing up." I went in to pinch his cheeks, but he artfully dodged me. I tried to contain my vicarious excitement and be cool about it.

"Hey shut up! I changed a lot over the summer."
We agreed to go to lunch to catch up. We went to our respective rooms, showered, changed and left the apartment. I took Kate's car with her permission and drove us to The Palm Court, a nice restaurant nearby. As we ate, Parker asked if I was going to VVHS' homecoming game. The game was one of the few fun things to do in town for VVHS students and alumni alike. But to be honest, with everything I had going on, I hadn't thought about it much. Of course, to my brother it was elementary. I should go because he was going. Never mind the fact that he was a senior and a very popular one at that. My time at VVHS reached its sunset, I had no reason to go back. Still, Parker spent the better half of our meal trying to convince me to go. I always had a hard time saying no to my little brother. Besides I figured Leona probably wouldn't be there. She hardly cared for attending games when we were students at VVHS. "Ok count me in. So how is the school sponsored internship going?"

"Oh, I got fired."

"They fired you from Gap?" I was in disbelief.

"Yep. My boss said I dress like a hobo and I'm unapproachable"

"He said you dress like a hobo?"

"Well not really. He said I dress oddly. What a way to fire someone."
Parker didn't care about the internship at all. It was supposed to be a way to make up credits he needed to graduate, but he wasn't concerned with graduation either. I had encouraged him to take the internship seriously, but it was hard not to laugh at him being fired. Students rarely ever got fired from these school sponsored gigs. Short of stealing from the register or shoplifting, all other transgressions were

forgivable. The businesses that participated in the program knew the interns were a temporary nuisance and put up with them to help the school. It was all about being a supportive institution within the community.

"You know Kate's going to flip. You needed those credits to walk the stage."

"I can always do a summer of home school."

"You're so badass." We both chuckled and I swirled my fork around the food on my plate. I do that a lot. I don't know why I do. I just do. It feels comfortable for some reason - my swirling my fork. Besides it really seems to irritate Kate, so of course I've made no effort to stop myself from doing it. We finished eating and headed back to Kate's car. We turned up the radio and took the freeway. There was absolutely nothing like witnessing us in that moment. I was driving at 75 miles per hour, while practically screaming along to whatever song came on with Parker doing the same from the passenger seat. We were all smiles, all light-heartedness, and it was fantastic. Spending that time with my brother, a simple a lunch and a car ride, was as close to truly happy as I had been in months.

November 9, 2009

Today I called Alessandra. We had another tryst, after we both finished our afternoon classes. This time it was at Montclair Park. We kissed. I kissed her neck, then her breasts.

She whispered, "take me." We kissed again. I told her I couldn't because I'd forgot to bring protection. She sighed. She ran her hands across my chest, and down my abs. We kissed yet again, and I stroked her hair as she went down on me. We stopped and left only after Tiffany and Evan, who had also come along again, informed us that the park rangers were making their rounds. On the car ride back, Alessandra told me Ramsey said he loved her.

This more than surprised me a little bit, since up until then I was under the impression that they're relationship was all tangled in hypothetical thoughts. If he wasn't afraid of commitment, they'd be together. If he felt like he could trust, he would pursue something. Then I recalled how she told me she wasn't ready to have sex at Josslyn's party, but then asked me to take her tonight. It was possible she had just progressed since then, but this new thing with Ramsey adding a new confusing dimension to an already less than desirable situation. I felt like we should probably stop seeing each other. She must have sensed something was amiss.

Before I could even say anything, she asked me not to stop seeing her because of it. "I like what we have going here," she said. Confusing was an understatement. Chaos was an understatement. I told her I wouldn't but as I exited Evan's car, I told myself I'd break it off with her the next time we saw each other. This was all getting to be too convoluted. I was certain she was playing some kind of mind games and at first, I found it hot, but now it was exhausting.

November 12, 2009

Today was big game day. That's what everyone calls homecoming game here, remember? I woke up, went to school and when I got back around 4:00 pm, I headed straight to my room and to my closet. High up on a shelf next to the folded stacks of sweaters and pants, I kept a sleek black shoebox. I opened it up, pushed past the pictures, pins, and other little mementos, until I found and pulled out two silver and black beaded necklaces. Silver and black were Villa Valle High's school colors. I had a great time wearing these. I wore them to pep rallies, soccer matches, lacrosse games, and most important to the homecoming game - the big game between Villa Valle and our cross-town rivals Truman High. I laid the beads down on my bed and closed the box. Then I went into the bathroom to get ready.

I emerged dressed in a black button-down shirt and slim fit blue jeans. I put on black dress-style socks to match and my favorite gray slip on shoes. I don't know what it is, but I've always enjoyed coordinating my clothes a certain way. It makes me feel like Cary Grant for some reason. I walked to meet with Lexie at our favorite sandwich shop and we lunched and laughed until about six o'clock. I walked her home, and then walked back to the apartment where Parker greeted me upon entry. Parker was wearing a striped shirt, thin zip up sweater, and black jeans.

"Are you ready?" Parker said.

"Of course," I said, "but wait one second." That's when I went up to my room and picked up the two beaded necklaces from off the bed. I walked back down the stairs and towards the living room where Parker stood awaiting anxiously. "Ok so I've had these since my freshman year I think, and I want to give you one. I had the best times wearing these. And now that I've graduated, I don't really need two."

"It's like the passing of the scepter," Parker said. His eyes lit up wide with enthusiasm. It was cool having someone look up to me.

"Something like that," I said chuckling a bit. I placed the beads around his neck and stepped back. "Looking good kiddo."

"Thanks Col," replied Parker. We headed to the school, which was only a couple blocks away in walking distance. When we got inside, we went straight to the field. As we paid for our tickets, we could hear cheers and jeers emitting from the junior varsity game, which was ending. Once we paid, we entered the large chain- link gateway to the home side of the bleachers.

"Truman is totally going to lose," said Parker.

"Oh totally," I said.

"Hey Parker, hey Colin you guys made it," said a familiar voice. I turned around to discover it was Amelia Persini. Amelia is pretty, 5'4", petite, with narrow, sensuous lips, and big light brown eyes. Her hair is smooth, dark, and cut to her jaw line - a sharp contrast from how it flowed down her back when she and I first met. Oh, before I forget to mention, Amelia was my high school girlfriend. Anyway, she stared at me and said, "well aren't you going to hug me darling?" I laughed and obliged.

"It's been so long," I said, not really knowing what else to say. We were off and on for most school until junior year. That's when we broke up for good. She's hands-down the most stylish girl I've ever dated. She was wearing a red coat with a black t-shirt, blue jeans, and black ballet flats. In her hair she wore a bright red headband with a big bow on the side of it, to match her coat. We were high up in the bleachers. I took a seat and Amelia sat down right in my lap. This would have been surprising if we weren't both notorious flirts and our history hadn't brought us close enough to be able to do such things without much thought behind it.

"Where's Parker?" I asked, having just noticed my brother took off.

"Over there, see that little circle of seniors and girls," Amelia noted.

"Ah, that's my boy," I said.

"So, what's this I hear about you hooking up with a girl from Sacred Heart?" Amelia said. It was an abrupt transition. Since I wasn't her boyfriend anyone, it also wasn't any of her business, but I figured I'd play along.

"Who told you?" I asked.

"Heard it through the grapevine," she said. She was sitting in my lap.

She smiled cheekily, then turned towards me and grew serious for a second. "Was this Sacred Heart girl a better kisser than me?" she asked.

"Of course not," I said. I wasn't obligated to reassure her, but I wanted to. She turned back around and continued watching the game. I wrapped his arms around her. She was so soft, so warm, so familiar, yet after a few minutes she got up and sat one stand behind me. "What happened?" I asked.

"That was just... a little too comfortable," she said.
I decided to lean back and rest my head on her knees. Amelia put her arms around my neck and held me there. We stayed that way for the remainder of the first quarter. Around the start of the second quarter, a blonde girl with honey-colored eyes, accompanied by a slightly taller redhead approached us.

"You two are back together, again? I see some things really do never change," said the girl in a snotty tone. Her name was Sienna Arliss, and she was Amelia's nemesis, for lack of a better term. They graduated class of '09 together, just one year behind me. Sienna was known for being easy and a heavy cocaine user. I'm sure you had heard about her. She's also a merciless gossip and a snob despite it all, which is in part how she got to be Amelia's nemesis in the first place. The other part had to do with their mutual ex-boyfriend, Nick, but that's another story entirely.

"Well, you're still a scathing bitch, so you're right not much has changed."

"Not that it's any of your business, but we're just here as friends," I said.

"Is that why you two are all cuddled up?" asked Sienna.

"Not everyone who touches a guy, sleeps with him. Just you," Amelia said. At that point I couldn't help but laugh. Sienna's face turned red hot. Amelia always got the best of her. "You wish you could get as much action as I do," Sienna said.

"Please not even a porn star would want as much action as you get," Amelia quipped. I pitied Sienna. There was no coming back from that. Normally I would've stayed out it and just observed, but she had never been nice to me or anyone really.

"And they get paid at least twice your rate," I added. I couldn't resist. Amelia laughed and Sienna's friend finally spoke up, which probably wasn't the best idea.

"You two are supposed to be cool?" the friend said. "You're just coming off as vicious haters." She flipped her hair and threw her nose into the air.

"Correction honey, we are cool and who allowed you to speak anyway?" said Amelia. She was always so matter of fact when she was irritated. It was both a little scary and a little hot. Since I had already joined in on the conversation I figured why stop now?

"Yeah Sienna, get control of your sidekick before she gets in over her head. Then go terrorize Tokyo or whatever it is you do all day," I said.

"You two are so not worth my time," Sienna said. She flipped her hair and signaled to her friend that it was time to leave.

"Bye, don't come back anytime soon," Amelia shouted as they walked away. She slowly released her arms from around my neck.

"What?" was all I managed to say this time.

"Sienna had a point," Amelia said. "We're not together anymore."
Just then Kelly walked up to us. "Remember me?" she said. "We met the other night at The Ruby." I didn't recognize her at first and paused.

"Kelly, right?" I said trying to sound casual. I remembered her alright.

"Wow, you remembered," Kelly said sarcastically.

"I'm good with names," I gloated, ignoring her sarcasm. I then stood up and gave her a light, but friendly hug. She commented on my cologne. I told her it was Burberry Brit and we all sat down. She was too young to date, but that didn't mean I couldn't be friendly. "How have you been?" I asked her.

"Good, I didn't expect to see you here though. Is this your..." Kelly started.

"Ex-girlfriend, Amelia? Why yes, it is." I interrupted.

Amelia rolled her eyes at me. "Hi," she said to Kelly.

"Kelly care to stay?" I asked. I don't know why, I just blurted it out. Maybe I thrive on chaos. The tension was so thick you could cut it with a butter knife.

"Sure," Kelly said waving over a few friends. "You guys don't mind if my friends come sit with us, do you?"

"Of course not," I said even though I very much minded. I would have rather been alone with Amelia, but there I was ruining the moment again. There were three other girls who came over with Kelly. They were all tall, thin, cute volleyball players. Amelia detested them instantly, although she stayed with me until the beginning of half-time. That's when her gay best friend Mark called.

"Hi cutie," Mark said to me smiling.

"Hey Mark," I replied in a flirty voice. I couldn't help it. I liked the attention I got from Mark. He knew it and I knew dishing out a few compliments wasn't hurting anyone. It's not like anything was going to happen with Mark. It was totally safe.

"Well, we're off to get drunk with my boyfriend," Amelia said.

She was trying to make me jealous. "Aw without me?" I said.

"Oh yeah, cause you coming wouldn't be awkward at all," Amelia said.

"It's Colin, he's never awkward," Mark said.

"Thanks for the vote of confidence Mark," I said. "See Mark wants me there." I was teasing. The last thing I wanted to do was go hang out with Amelia and her new boyfriend. I did however want to push the envelope. I wanted to see far Amelia would bend before she snapped.

"It's not Mark I'm worried about," she said.

"Ok, we'll have fun and be safe babe," I said. The last part was a reflex. Maybe Sienna really did have a point about us being too comfortable with each other.

"Ok, bye," she said. She gave me a big hug. We stared into each other's eyes for a second and I leaned in for a kiss. Amelia almost let me and then stepped back. Mark had turned his head for a second to say hi to a cheerleader missed the whole thing. When he turned back, he hugged me too, and he and Amelia left.

"He totally called you babe," Mark whispered.

"I know, but whatever," Amelia replied. I shook the whole thing off and focused my attention on Kelly. She was laughing along with one of her friends. I joined in on the conversation. Within minutes I was telling jokes and dispensing advice about guys, as the girls listened intently. In that time span I was asked to the homecoming dance by a very adorable freshman and invited to two after parties. If I was still a student at the school, I would have said yes. Before we knew it half time was over. I received a text asking where I was. I didn't recognize the number. I'd replied that I'd love to tell them, but that first I'd like to know who I was speaking to.

Turns out, it was Chloe, Kasey's friend. He gave Chloe my number. They were at the game and inviting me to come hang with them. I thought about it for a second. I got up and gave Kelly and her friends each hugs goodbye. I walked across the stands in between and around groups of teens and couples cuddling in the cold November air. I looked around but still didn't see them, so I pulled out my phone and sent a text asking where they were exactly. As I waited for their reply, something else struck me - remorse. "Hey Amelia, I'm sorry about earlier ...I guess I just miss you sometimes." A few seconds passed. My phone vibrated to signal I had received a response back.

"I understand, and it's no big deal," Amelia wrote.

"You sure?"

"Yeah."

I knew her well enough to know she meant it and it was as if all the tension that had filled my bones prior to sending it left. I was flooded with relief. After that Chloe sent a text giving me their exact location. *Top left corner of the stands, passed the marching band.* As I approached, they shouted my name. I walked up, hugged Chloe then Adrienne, who was with her boyfriend Owen, and then Kasey.

"Looking sexy in that marching band uniform Kase," I said.

"You're on drugs if you think this is sexy," Kasey replied.

The only thing he hated more than being in marching band was the uniform. It wasn't always that way he used to love it. I'd guess social pressure made him hate it. He was only still participating in it to finish out the year and make his mom happy. We all laughed and watched the rest of the game together. Out of nowhere, Chloe grabbed my hand casually and held it. I squeezed hers back. We held hands for a good portion of the third quarter before she broke the clasp to clap at yet another touchdown. Villa Valle ended up winning the game 54 to 19. Everyone on our side celebrated. I turned to Chloe, who was standing right next to me, and hugged her tight. After breaking the embrace, we each returned to cheering just as loudly as anyone else. As the cheers died down the stands began to empty. Chloe, Adrienne, Owen and I made our way down the steps and towards the exit on the home side of the field. I ran into Parker and a group of his friends as they reached the last rung.

"We're going to eat, want to come?" I asked.

"It's alright. I'm going to hang out with Cherri," he said smiling. Just then one of his friends leaned in and to invite me to a homecoming afterparty. I gave a noncommittal answer and then hugged my brother goodbye. He was already much more responsible than I was at his age, so I didn't have to worry about him getting into trouble. The cold night air swept in and made me shiver. As Chloe, Kasey, and the crew made our way to an old-fashioned hamburger shop just up the street from VVHS. Students from both Villa and Truman High were there, but surprisingly everyone coexisted rather nicely. As we walked in, I could hear the chatter about the game, homecoming kings and queens, and plans for the dance. We all walked over to the counter, stood in line, and ordered a short time later. After about thirty minutes, Kasey and Chloe got their food. A few minutes later Adrienne, Owen, and I got ours.

"They forgot to give me a straw," I noticed getting up to go retrieve one.

"Can you get me one too please?" Adrienne asked.

"But of course love," I answered. I rose from my seat and walked over towards the condiments counter. That's when I saw her. She appeared just as she had in my dream. The only difference was her outfit. She was dressed in a black cardigan, white ruffled shirt, a tight black mini-dress, and her favorite ballet flats. It's funny how when you really get to know someone you end up remember everything about them, even their favorite shoes. I weighed out my options. I could either go back to the table without the condiments and create an undoubtedly awkward situation or confront her head on. *To hell with it,* I thought. I walked right up to her and started a conversation.

"Hi Leona. You're looking well," I said. I realize how pretentious that must have sounded now, but it was the only thing I could muster up enough courage to say.

"Hey! Thanks babe. How have you been?" she said smiling.

"Good, how have you been?" I said trying to remain casual.

"Oh, I've been great, work is shit, but aside from that great."

We stood there making small talk for about five whole minutes. I would have been upset that she was standing there talking to me like nothing had ever changed between us, but I knew her too well. She was raw, unfiltered, and usually oblivious when her words hurt someone else's feelings, unless told directly. In those rare times when she was aware of an issue, she was the kind to ignore it and move on. So, I played along. I stood there responding to her, laughing occasionally, and pretending everything was alright. After a little while, she left, and I went back to my table. I tried to brush it off, but I must have seemed tense because Chloe placed her hand on my knee and started caressing my back. I can't lie, it was soothing.

"We're all going to go back to my place to watch a movie. Are you in?" I agreed and the next thing I knew we were all drinking Malibu rum in Chloe's garage. Chloe and I were seated on a large sofa. Adrienne and Owen were seated right next to us. All of us were kissing except Kasey. He was seated on the far end of the sofa, trying not to so seem too un-amused. Chloe broke our kiss and looked me dead in the eyes.

"I really want to go down on you," she said brazenly.

I was excited but confused. "We've been through this before," I replied.

"Okay, but this time I'm ready," she said.

"You sure?" I said. I didn't want to push her into anything she didn't genuinely want to do. I would have been fine with just a handjob. Hell, I would have been fine just sitting there. She seemed so unsure of herself the last time we were together.

"Yes ...wait, no. I'm nervous." There was that uncertainty rearing its head.

"Let's just watch the movie then."

"That means, we have to just watch the movie too," scoffed Owen.

Now it was Adrienne's turn to try not to look too un-amused. We turned our attention back to the television screen in front of us. I noticed Kasey seemed to be dozing off. I also noticed Chloe's hand hadn't left its spot on my inner thigh. She crept up to the top of my waist and undid my pants underneath the blanket that lap across both of our legs.

"Wait, I have to go to the restroom, wouldn't want to ruin the moment by accidentally giving you a golden shower," I said kind of laughing. Owen laughed too and so did Adrienne and Kasey. Chloe just said to hurry back. I walked outside the garage and into Chloe's house. Once I had found and was safely inside the bathroom I called Lexie. It felt like the phone rang forever before she answered.

"Hey," she said, calm and cool.

"Fuck, fuck, fuck," was all I managed to say.

"What's happening? Where are you?"

I was sweating bullets. I had hooked up before, why was this any different? Chloe was old enough. She was pretty and sweet, but she was also uncertain. It seemed to be like she was vacillating between curiosity sex and feeling pressured to delve into the act to keep up with Adrienne. I couldn't shake that feeling. "I'm at Kasey's friend, Chloe's house. We were all in the garage watching a movie until she said she wants to go down on me. Now I'm in the bathroom calling you."

"Oh my god, you would!" Lexie laughed, then she pivoted to being serious. "How do you feel about that?"

"I don't know." I lied. I couldn't tell her the truth. I wanted to go back into the garage and hook up with Chloe. I wanted to be cool and carefree. Yet, I was simultaneously looking for a reason not to.

"What don't you know?"

"On one hand she's 18, which is only a year younger than us. On the other she's still in high school and there's still a lot she doesn't know about herself. I don't want to be one of those assholes who picks up younger girls because I know they're impressionable and I can easily have sex with them."

"Then don't be. You have a choice," Lexie said.

She was right, but the solution wasn't that simple to me. A nagging voice in my head kept telling me that I'd be a chump to follow her advice. You remember what I was like back in high school. Sex was a big deal to me, until I got it out of the way. I was feeling myself slip into old habits. "I know, but I'm torn here. How the hell do I walk into a garage full of people and turn down a hot girl? What if I end up hurting her feelings? I'll look like an idiot. I vowed to stop missing opportunities after Leona. I don't want to go back to being the way I was when things happened with her. But if I do this, what does that make me?"

"That's complicated. I can't answer that for you. All I can do is tell you to think about it. I mean really think. Only you know the answer to this. Only you know what you want to do. So, ask yourself and go with that. I know you'll come to the right decision."

"Alright," I said, then I thanked her for her listening and hung up. I knew I didn't want to take advantage of Chloe or this situation, but I still didn't know exactly how I was going to get out of it. I walked back to the garage knowing that if I took anymore time, they were going to come look for me.

"That was a very long piss," Owen said as I came in.

"Sorry," I said. As soon as I sat back down Chloe placed her hand on my inner thigh again. This time took things a step further and she slid it inside the waistband of my boxer-briefs. Before I knew it, she had begun touching me bare. I should have said something. I should stopped it somehow, but I didn't. *So much for all that rumination.*

"Can we start with this?" Chloe whispered.

"No objections here," I managed to say. I decided to give in. I don't know what changed between when I hung up with Lexie and returned from the bathroom, but I had abandoned any moral quandaries that stood in the way.

Chloe continued until we heard a car pull into the driveway.

"Shit your mom's home!" said Adrienne.

"Oh fuck," said Chloe. I was relieved, so I said nothing. We finished the movie, no touching, no innuendos, just us and the film. Then, looking at the time, we all realized we should get going. Owen left first and then Kasey's mom arrived to pick him up. I decided to excuse myself around the same time. On the way Lexie sent me a text message. It was a picture of a post it that I wrote her in the 11th grade. It read, "I don't know what happened to make you upset, but whatever it is I hope it changes for the better." I read it again and again. I wondered how I had changed so drastically. Was I still that same guy, deep down inside? Was I still the same guy who bought Amelia chocolates for no reason when we were dating? The same guy who wrote love letters to her almost every day and later wrote that note to Lexie. Was I still that Colin Prescott? Surely not.

I had let the disappointment mount and turn me into this cynical, unrecognizable, *monster*. I began to shake a bit just at the thought. My head began to spin. I stopped to regain my composure. Not caring about my clothes, I hoisted myself up on a nearby half-wall which surrounded the front of a large Tudor. The wind blew, the sky grew dark, and I lit a cigarette. By the time I finished smoking, I'd stopped shaking. But I couldn't stop thinking about it. I hated that moment. I was filled with remorse. *What the hell is wrong with me?* I sat there for what seemed like hours. Eventually, as all predicaments do, things grew calm. I played "Way Out" by the Yeah Yeah Yeahs on the walk home to soothe me.

November 13, 2009

Leo called me to invite me to a beach bonfire party. When I said I didn't have a way to get there, he offered to pick me up. I'd be riding with him Lily, and Ezra. Before we hung up, he mentioned that Levi Sahid would be at the party, as a guarantee that things would be wild. Now Levi Sahid is notorious for three things: hard partying, constant nudity, and hooking up with everyone he can, and I mean everyone. It took me about 10 minutes to get ready and by then Lily, Leo, and Ezra were downstairs. There have been many girls in my life, but none of them were quite like Lily Wilding.

She's warm, but direct. She's intellectual, but not condescending. She has phenomenal taste in music, she knows all the best places to get great vegan foods (though she isn't even a vegan), she's the kind of girl you could call at 1am and take on a spontaneous car ride to anywhere. At 5'5," with shoulder length curly auburn hair, and green eyes, she wasn't bad to look at either. I adored her for all of this. But of course, she was perfectly immune to my charms, which made me adore her even more.

We've known each other since sophomore year at VVHS and built a friendship over the years. She got me to listen to Elliott Smith and took me to his memorial wall. She was there when I first learned how to drive, when I first flirted his way out of a fender bender shortly after and threw his first college party at my mother's apartment. Now she was there waiting for me to get into her dad's car so we could all go to the beach. I walked through the lobby and down the stairs in front of the apartment building.

"We've been expecting you Mr. Prescott," Lily said jokingly through the lowered passenger seat window. I got in the car, and we took off. As Leo turned up the music, Lily turned around and pulled a little bag from her purse.

"Who's down to road toke?" she asked.

"Lighting up to the Sex Pistols? Hell yeah!" I said.

"Ding, ding, ding you knew the name of the band," Lily said. "You get the first bowl." She packed some of the cannabis into the mouth of her blue glass pipe.

"You guys really didn't know this was "Liar" by the Sex Pistols?" I asked.

"I thought it might have been them, but Ezra had us convinced it was Black Flag," Leo said. He chucked a pillow at Ezra.

"No way, Black Flag had a totally different sound. Johnny Rotten's voice is so distinct," I said. I can only imagine how annoying I must've sounded. I hated music snobs, yet there I was being one.

"Yeah whatever, just take a hit," Ezra said. He was a bit embarrassed, but he had no reason to be. We can't know everything. That's part of being human.

"Hey, don't be a sore loser Ezra," Lily said mocking.

I took a slow long drag from the pipe, held in my breath for a couple minutes then exhaled. Thick white smoke permeated the air. I passed the pipe to Ezra when I was done, and he did the same before passing it to Lily. By the time they we had all taken quite a few turns, Leo included (which was a bit of a juggling act on his part), the music had changed to the mellow sounds of 311. "I know a drugstore cowgirl so afraid of getting bored," we all sang loudly. Ezra was sitting with his head thrown back against the seat and I leaned my head against the window, my body spread out diagonally. I sat up when Leo rolled down all the windows so we could air out.

A cool breeze flooded the car, taking the smoke inside with it. We got on the highway, blasting the music and singing along semi-accurately until we reached the beach. Leo parked in a lot just inches from the shore. We all got out of the car, grabbed the supplies from the trunk, and ran merrily towards the glowing pit with our friends around it. If they hadn't been waving their arms in the air to signal us, I'm not sure we would have found them though. We so were incredibly stoned. When we reached the group, everyone exchanged hellos and hugs. As we settled in, I noticed Leona was there. The events that transpired between us suddenly seemed silly. My cynicism and transformation were all justified. I could never go back to the sap I used to be. The one Lexie admired. I wouldn't let that happen.

"Colin, I didn't know you were coming?" Leona said.

"Really?" I said sarcastically. I wasn't friendly the way I had been when we'd first ran into each other. Honestly, I was too high to care.

"Um yes, I really didn't know you were coming. Is everything alright?"

"Yes," I said quickly, then I stopped and thought about it. I took her arm in mine and walked her a few feet away from everyone else. "Actually no, everything's not alright. You shattered my heart into a million little goddamn pieces and now you're just pretending everything is cool. News flash, it's not, I'm not, we're not," I declared.

"Maybe we should talk about this when you're not high," Leona said staring into my eyes which I later discovered were a glassy and red.

"It doesn't matter that I'm high. I've been dying to tell you this either way," I said. The conviction in my voice shocked even me.

"Oh, well I don't know what to say?"

"Of course you don't," I said. "In fact, I don't even need you to say anything, it's just...I saw us. I saw us together, and happy, despite everything. And you kept me around for the attention. You joked about marrying me and said I was the perfect guy for you. We had moments, special moments, tons of special fucking moments. We were real and flawed, yet we worked so well together. I guess the problem is I was the only one of us who could see that."

"I'm sorry," Leona said. Those were the words I had been dying to hear since the night I told her how I felt this past summer. The night she broke what was left of my heart into a million pieces. I'd finally told her I was into her, and she said, and I quote 'it's too late, get over it.' I sat there for a while on her living room floor, sipping my beer and trying to keep it together. What did she mean by it's too late? How could she be so callous to say to just get over it. I walked the three miles home, stripped of my resolve, my confidence, my hope. She was so cold in that moment. She had never been cold with me. I didn't know why this was happening or what to do.

All the little signs that normally point to someone liking you, were there. But she didn't feel that. With those three words "get over it," she'd cut me wide open. I hadn't healed and I didn't think I ever would. I wanted her more than anything else in the world, but she didn't want me. It pained me, deeply, but that was the reality.

Not everyone you're attracted to is going to be attracted to you. I wasn't into Kasey for example, and I didn't view myself as a villain for it. Yet I had villainized Leona this entire time for not requiting my feelings.

I knew this logically, but I couldn't make sense of it emotionally before then. Now that we were staring each other down and the truth was laid out bare, I realized how ridiculous I'd been acting. Did I ever truly love her or was I just massively self-involved? Do I even know what love is? Why am I so desperate to be loved? I wanted to recoil, to retract everything I'd said to her moments ago. All I could focus on was that not being vulnerable in front of her ever again.

"Don't be," I said. "Now that it's all out there, I think I'll be fine."

"Can we go back to being friends now?" she asked.

"Yeah, sure," I said. I meant it. We weren't ever going to be as close as we once were for obvious reasons, but we could absolutely be friends. I didn't see the harm in building back a friendship. We were friends first after all.

"Good, because I missed you," she said.

I couldn't help but let out a little laugh, then I took a breath. "Yeah, me too," I said. I meant that as well. It was excruciating and yet a huge relief to have that conversation. Everything had finally been laid out in the open. Lily walked over to me a short while later and asked if I was ok. She could always sense when something was off with me. I told her I was just adding another chapter to my autobiography.

"Memoirs of an Emotional Masochist," I said.

"Sounds promising," Lily joked. I laughed a real laugh this time. We walked back to rejoin the crowd together, which had grown a bit since we arrived, and both grabbed beers. Everyone gathered around in small circles and shared different stories. There was one about a girl from Villa Community, who tried seducing her Poli Sci Professor only to discover he had erectile dysfunction. One about a guy who was caught having sex with his girlfriend by her grandmother. Oh, and that one story about the rich girl most of us knew, who ran away and became an exotic dancer.

Besides that, there were the typical conversations. *Colin, I swear saw you at*

the White Party last Friday. Lily, are you going to the warehouse party this Saturday?
Somewhere around this time I had become bored with just standing around and started
dancing. Lily looked bored too, so I grabbed her hand. We danced around aimlessly.
Soon people started to join us. We all danced and sang along to the songs emanating
from the radio Leo had brought along. Levi Sahid had arrived and took a small group
skinny dipping at some point, but surprisingly nobody paid much attention to that. Lily
and I had everyone on their feet. We closed the night eating s'mores and drinking wine.
It felt nice.

November 14, 2010

I slept for the half the day and woke up still hung-over. I was determined to go on with my normal routine. I went for a walk, drank coffee with Lexie at Café Insomnia, and ended up heading across the street to Montclair Park by myself afterwards. It was around 7:00 pm. The hangover had faded by then, but nothing seemed any clearer. I pressed play on the mp3 player I always kept in his pocket and walked down the narrow path that led into the park from the entrance. I walked slowly across the park and sat on the swing set.

Then something just came over me, I selected Courtney Love's band Hole from the menu, and rocketed myself as "Malibu" by Hole blasted through my earphones. With each verse I propelled myself harder and higher. It was as if somehow all his thoughts, troubles, worries vanished into the air. I was no longer at the park, no longer part of anything solid, I was taking flight. My body swayed with the swing. My feet could no longer even graze the soft white sand below. And I just started signing. I sang until I laughed, I laughed until he cried, and eventually I sat there still. I thought about everything that had happened over the past year.

I could hear it all. I could hear Kate jeering me for not being at a university, not living up to my potential. Dad's calm voice telling me to relax over the phone, Traci telling me to ignore our mother and listen to our father, the strum of Parker's guitar. I was bitter about some of the setbacks in my life, the lack of empathy, that he wanted empathy. And I was admittedly jealous of the attention Kate was giving my brother. She hadn't given me one ounce of attention, except for when I'd made a mistake of course. So odd that she saw me as completely flawed and Kasey and the others as perfect. I was neither and both. In that one moment I felt more human than I had ever felt before, and I hated it.

So, I did the only thing I knew would help me forget, I called Lily up, went over to her place and Leo, Ezra, and I all got stoned. It was a complete mental vacation, lying there on Lily's bedroom floor, with "Just" by Radiohead streaming through her stereo and right into my soul. I began to laugh, first it was at my hands, then the destruction my impaired mind realized they had caused and could cause. With every touch of a girl's skin, every sprit of my favorite cologne, every intimate hug - they were committing evil. They were drawing others in only so the rest of me could let them down. They were devils, those hands of mine. Then I laughed at the word devils. I laughed at the meaning of the word and the sound. All of it was hilarious to me.

Meanwhile, Lily was spacing out, Leo was laughing with me (although Leo didn't know why), and Ezra was eating almonds like he'd just discovered what they were. It was magic. The next thing I saw was the sun shining in through the thin pale cream curtains that hung about Lily's giant bedroom window. I rose to a halfway sitting position from the spot where I'd lain and looked around. Ezra has passed out with the almonds right beside him. Leo was snuggling Lily's favorite pink stuffed horse, and Lily was lying face down on her bed with one arm hanging off the side. I ran a hand over my face. I sat up completely, then gradually stood and walked out of Lily's room and across a long dark hall. At the end of the hall was the bathroom. I opened the door, turned the cold silver knobs on the sink and watched the water rush out of the faucet. I rinsed my face, dried it with a nearby hand towel and left the bathroom. Smoothening out the wrinkles my clothes, I walked back towards Lily's room. I opened the door ever so carefully, tip-toed to her desk and found a bunch of post its. I grabbed a pen and wrote a note before I went home that read:

Thanks for the amazing time. You were very sexy (all three of you!) call me.

All of my love,
CP

November 21, 2009

The strangest thing happened yesterday. There's this guy I know named Duncan. He's tall, with light brown hair, an actor's smile, and a football player's build. I met him through his girlfriend in October. I didn't write about it because I meet people all the time and nothing notable happened. After learning about the Jeff and Stella debacle, Duncan and his girl made a few jokes about me joining them for a three-way, but that was it. It was a jest, all in good fun. So yeah, nothing notable happened, until last Friday.

On Friday, my friend Emmett invited me to a party at his house. I met Emmett last year, but he's been friends with Duncan forever, so of course Duncan and his girlfriend were invited as well. By the time I received the text I had already been drinking. Duncan offered me a ride, despite the fact that Emmett lived walking distance from me. I didn't think much of it at the time, but that should have been my first clue that something was off.

When Duncan came to pick me up, I noticed that his girlfriend wasn't in the car. *No big deal,* I thought. I know she doesn't really enjoy parties. We arrived at Emmett's, and I kept drinking. As more guests arrived, I switched from beers to hard liquor. Eventually, Emmett, Lily, Ezra, and I smoked a bowl in Emmett's room. I met some new people, told a few jokes, and somehow (I don't exactly remember how) I ended up in Emmett's room alone with Duncan. We sat there and just talked for a while. He exchanged stories about our lives and relationships.

I learned that he had an ultraconservative Christian upbringing, which I could related to being from a Catholic West Indian family. He confided in me that things weren't going so well with his girlfriend, though they seemed happy on the surface. I opened up about my disaster of a dating life and he made a joke or two about me being too sexy to deal with any bullshit. I decided to boldly return the compliment and then the room grew still. He rose to his feet and abruptly suggested that we take off our shirts. I wasn't quite sure where this was going, but I didn't really care.

I was entrenched in living in the moment. Next, he suggested we take off our pants. I was still game. I don't remember exactly what I was thinking or what I expected to happen from there, but I knew I was all in. Oddly enough, we just stood there staring at each other in our boxer-briefs. It wasn't an overly sexualized moment. I was drunk and high, but I could tell at least that little bit. Instead, it felt like when two kids play 'I'll show you mine, if you show me yours.' We stood there bare skinned with the streetlights from the outside hitting us through Emmett's bedroom window.

Duncan had faint tan lines, and a scar here and there. I thought he was absolutely beautiful. We just stood there giggling like two drunken kids. Things must've gotten a little too real for him at that point, because he interrupted with another musing. Even drunk I could tell he was struggling to think of his next move.

"Not sure what to do next. I didn't think I'd get this far," he said. He blushed when he said it. I wanted to ask what he wanted to happen. If I'm being honest, I would have maybe kissed him. I know he has a girlfriend, but they don't really seem to be on the same page. I don't know. He ended up daring me run downstairs with him to freak everyone out. I obliged. I thought was a funnier idea than it actually was, because of the alcohol. After shaking hands with a room full of people, while only in our underwear, we went back upstairs.

As we redressed, we intermittently made eye contact. When we got back downstairs everyone had begun a drinking game. Duncan lost a round and was dared to give me a lap dance. He turned bright red and backed out of the dare. He did however, text me yesterday making a bunch of sexual jokes. I went along with it. I don't exactly know why, but I did. I don't think there needs to be a reason to. Whatever flirtation we have going seems to be in jest. Girlfriend or not, if he wanted things to go further, he would have made a move on me at that party. Besides, I wasn't sure I was ready for anything to happen. Kasey was the only guy I had kissed and look how that turned out.

November 28, 2009

Duncan and I sent text messages to each other all week. The conversations were pretty normal, save a few sexual jokes. But it's really nothing any of my other guy friends and I don't joke about. It seems to me like he's just comfortable with himself. Anyway, we ran into each other at the Village yesterday. He told me he and his girlfriend broke up. He seemed pretty upset about it. We talked for a while, before he left for an appointment. I hope ends up okay.

In addition to this, my little brother Parker just reconnected with his best friend Brian. They went to Juilliard together, where they'd formed a two-man band called Boethius (yes named after the late philosopher). They decided to add a classmate of theirs from Villa Valle High named Max as their bassist. The three of them sound phenomenal together, but it's kind of hard to study for finals with them practicing so loudly in Parker's room. This is probably how Kate feels when I blast Nirvana's *Drain You* through my stereo.

December 9, 2009

School's a drag. It's finals week this week. I'm almost finished with my exams. I just have one left tomorrow, then I'm out for winter break, but God it's so daunting. Luckily Duncan and I have still been texting and casually hanging out. We kissed on a dare at a party last week. We were tipsy, but not drunk. I don't remember all the details, but I remember that the dare came from one of his friends. I thought Duncan was going to back out, but he got up without hesitation and leaned in to kiss me. I was riddled with anticipation. I wanted to know what the inside of his mouth tasted like.

My body coursed with excitement as our lips met. It wasn't just a quick peck either. It was a slow, intimate, kiss filled with authenticity. It felt like we sat there kissing forever, but it had to only be a minute or two. No one in the room seemed shocked. No one seemed to care much at all. I'm not really sure what to think about the kiss or Duncan but there's never a dull moment with this guy. I thought I was a flirt, but he makes me look like Mother Theresa.

Our conversations tend to vacillate from swapping mutual emotional support to trading compliments and sex jokes. The other day we met up after I got out of class. We went out to a place called Java Shoppe to get hot chocolate. I tried to get him to go to Café Insomnia, but he claimed he hates the people there. I wasn't sure if he was telling the whole truth. I suspected he might have had a fling with one of the baristas that ended badly. The point is we were at Java Shoppe, when he remarked that I was probably able to get any girl I wanted.

"Not the case," I said. I noticed I felt nervous as I responded.

"You must be kidding," he said. He lowered his eyes and raised an eyebrow in disbelief. I love when people speak and react to conversation with their whole bodies. I communicate in much the same way.

"No. I'm dead serious," I said. I knew my charms and I knew my limits. I couldn't figure out if he was just being friendly and jokingly flirty, or if he was really flirting with me. It was exhilarating and nerve-racking.

"Well, I don't believe you for a second, I mean look at you!"

"Stop exaggerating," I said pushing things a bit further.

"Who's exaggerating? You're charming, funny, smart, and good looking," he said. He was definitely flirting, that much was clear now.

"Oh please," I said. It was a genuine reaction. I adored and despised flattery.

"Oh, please yourself! You're incandescent," he said.

I had never been called incandescent before. I tried to think of a quick pun, but all I could come up with was to say I was decent at best. Something about Duncan made me nervous, but in a good way. I couldn't quite figure it out.

"More like ethereal at best," he quipped. He'd gotten me. I was putty in his hands in that moment. Men really are simply creatures. All you have to do to ensnare us is stroke our egos the right way. I was clearly no exception, and I clearly had a crush on this guy. I couldn't deny it any longer.

"Well, I thank you for the compliments, but I'm just another mere mortal."

"Please. You have no idea the things I've considered doing to you."

I paused. I wasn't expecting the conversation to go there. It was extremely bold of him, but also kind of sexy. I looked down at my iced coffee and smiled slightly when he said that. I was aware of my prowess. Though not infallible, I knew how to turn on the charm to get what I want. But I wasn't doing that now and it was still working. I found that kind of awesome. Then I realized what it was that he'd just said. I decided to pretend it was unimportant and change the subject. But I heard it, and it wasn't unimportant. I just can't figure out what it should mean, if anything. Sure, hearing that boosted my ego, made me smile, but I don't know. I've had very little faith in people who claim to be attracted to me since Leona.

Aside from that there's uneasiness in me about this situation that I just can't put my finger on. It has nothing to do with him being a guy. I'm starting to realize that gender doesn't really matter to me. It's something else. I can't seem to figure out when he's kidding and when he's serious. I don't want to look like a jackass by creating an unnecessary dramatic moment. It's better to say nothing.

Besides he's *very* attracted to women. I mean the guy's slept with almost every single girl in the Greater Los Angeles area. He also goes out to his way to hug me for a very long time, much longer than my other friends do. I catch him staring at me at random times and he's usually the first to initiate a dirty joke.

I'm not really sure what's going on and honestly, I'm not really sure he is either. He stumbles a lot. After he said what he said today he froze for a little while. Even after I changed the subject it took him a minute or so to get back into the natural flow of conversation. Remember that moment I told you about, when things got too real for him at Emmett's party? I'm starting to think that was another slip up. I think he knew he wanted to be alone and undressed with me, but he panicked once it was happening.

Looking back, I could see the wheels turning. I was drunk, but I still noticed the hesitation. I noticed that moment where he seemed to be searching his scattered thoughts for an idea before he declared we should run down the stairs. Running downstairs was something safe. Something to justify the whole predicament. I don't know. It doesn't change what a good friend he's become, and I need good friends. I don't think I should freak out or make a big scene about it. I don't think anyone should make a big scene when something like this happens. Sexuality is complicated. Attraction is complicated. I'm not worried about it.

December 18, 2009

You know how I said sexuality was complicated and that I wasn't worried? Well, I'm a little worried about it now. Last night I was out with Will at one of Parker's shows, when I got a text from Duncan that read *DTF?* In case you didn't know, DTF stands for down to fuck. I hadn't heard from Duncan since last week. I had sent him a friendly text, but he didn't respond. Emmett told me he does that a lot. He'll disappear, have loner moment, and reappear days later. That and apparently Duncan likes to start text conversations without finishing them.

"Sometimes, it'll be weeks before he gets back to anyone," Emmett said. "Last time I saw him though, he wouldn't stop talking about you." I wish I could say that was reassuring. Anyhow when I read Duncan's text, I couldn't believe it. I guess I shouldn't have been surprised given how things have been going. Part of me wanted to ask when and where. I simply said no in response.

He sent a text back that read, "oh shit, you're not Jenna." I didn't believe for a second that text was meant for someone named Jenna. Aside from the length of the names, Colin and Jenna aren't similar in the slightest. There's no way it was an accidental send. I decided to make normal conversation afterward, so he didn't feel too dejected or uncomfortable. I figured he'd been drinking or something, as it was Saturday night. Even if he hadn't been drinking, I know it must have taken some courage for him to ask. It wasn't the most respectful of questions, but it still took courage. Unfortunately, it feels I'm missing a piece to this puzzle. I can't shake this strange sinking sensation in my stomach. I spoke to Lexie about it, and she said I needed to look deeper, whatever that means.

December 22, 2009

It is now officially winter. I haven't really heard from Duncan since his DTF text. I tried inviting him to hang out with Ezra, Leo, and me but he didn't reply. There are three possibilities at play: either he's enjoying one of his intermittent loner moments like Emmett said, he's embarrassed, or he's being a dick because I turned him down. I've decided not to give a shit regardless. I must admit I felt a little ridiculous and naive, but that's over and done with. Someone told me they saw Duncan working as a go-go boy at a gay club in West Hollywood. I couldn't tell if it was true or not, but he does have the right physique for it. It would explain a lot actually, but I can't focus on that. He'll figure his feelings out. Maybe I'll see him again, maybe I won't. It doesn't matter.

In other news, I got a job at a trendy clothing store at the Village, called Pulse. I like it so far. Another plus is Kate has arranged for Parker's band, Boethius, to play a gig at a coffee shop in Seattle. She was able to do so through a friend of hers who happens to own the shop. Since we're all on winter vacation starting Monday, the timing worked out perfectly. Kate, Parker, Brian, and Max left for Washington this morning. This leaves me the run of the apartment for the next two weeks, though I should probably be praying for Parker instead of celebrating. That poor kid is going to be stuck with on a three-hour plane ride with our mother. I could hear the flight attendants begging for death in the bathroom already. I swear I'm going to jump out of the emergency exit, if that woman rings the bell one more time.

December 27, 2009

All I've done so far is work most afternoons and meet up with friends in the evening. When we meet up, we usually eat, then either go to this overlook on a hillside or to my place to drink and get stoned. We chose to go to the overlook on the hillside today and it was eventful to say the least. Ezra, Emmett, and I all drove up to Royale Drive. We could see the whole city for what seemed like miles. Ezra pulled out some banana bread and offered some to Emmett and me.

"It's got hash in it," he said and with that all three of us devoured our pieces. "It's a creeper, just so you know," Ezra added.

We sat back, legs crossed in front of us, just relaxing. Not high yet, not anything but sitting on a hillside taking in the beauty of the landscape. Then Ezra pulled out his pipe and filled it with a little the contents of a baggy, Emmett was holding.

"Get ready to enjoy some Purple Haze my friends," Emmett said.

"Like actual Purple Haze?" I asked.

"Yep, Hendrix certified," Ezra said, showing me the baggy with those two words, stamp with near the top of it. Ezra had a medical marijuana card and had been getting what he called prescription high for months. We completed a few sessions before we heard footsteps. The steps grew louder and louder, as if whoever was coming was running. We looked up quietly to the embankment above us and saw two well-dressed people, a man and a woman, who looked to be around our age.

The man turned to the woman and shouted: "look, isn't it beautiful?"

"Yes, it is," the woman agreed, pulling something towards her lips.

"Don't smoke that, you don't have time!" said the man.

"Okay, okay," said the woman.

"Let's go!" answered the man. With that the mysterious couple rushed away. We all turned to watch as they left. Emmett immediately insisted I go after them, and Ezra agreed. I resisted at first, but they persuaded me into it by plying me with compliments. Mere seconds had passed.

I jumped up from where I was seated and climbed up the embankment to chase the couple. However, when I reached the top, they had vanished. It would have been impossible for them to get away so fast. I was high, but I knew we hadn't taken long deliberating on whether I should follow them. I could have only been only a few minutes behind them max. Besides that, I didn't even see anyone running off, hear any footsteps, or hear a car taking off. It was as if the couple had never been there.

"Fucking impossible," I said aloud in pure disbelief. I continued to look around then turned to walk back down the embankment.

"What happened?" Ezra and Emmett said in unison.

"They aren't anywhere. I didn't hear a car take off. There's no way they could have run past the narrow ledge that leads out here at their speeds," I said.

"Oh crap," Emmett said. His eyes grew wide, and his jaw fell slack.

"Wait what did they say again?" Ezra said.

"You heard it too?" I said.

"I heard it too," Emmett joined in.

"Let's go. It's a sign," said Ezra.

With that we packed up what little we had brought with us and fled. We ran to the narrow ledge that led out to the hillside, walked across it prudently, and then jogged down the street to Emmett's car. On the way, we debated about whether what happened was real or we were just so stoned we had a group hallucination. I prefer to believe the latter. As Emmett sped down the road, something came over me. I lowered the window and yelled, "I feel infinite!" Emmett and Ezra both laughed.

"Isn't that from a book?" Emmett asked.

"Yep, The Perks of Being a Wallflower," I answered, "One of my favorites."

"Really?" Ezra said.

"Yeah, I know it's a sensitive novel and all, but yeah," I said, still very stoned.

"No, I meant I didn't know you read," Ezra said laughing.

"Yeah, when do you have time to read? You're such a whore," said Emmett.

"Shut up!" I said jokingly.

December 29, 2009

Today started off with things seeming normal. I woke up, got dressed, and went to at work at Pulse. The store claims it doesn't have a strict dress code, but there are several rules in place to the contrary. For example, the color of your hair must appear natural. Male employees must be clean shaven at all times and are not permitted to wear piercings or any other jewelry on the floor. Female employees are allowed to wear small studs in their ears, but makeup and nail polish must be toned down. The logic behind this is that we're supposed to be projecting the image of the All-American college kid. We're technically only required to imitate the looks they put out for the season, but the managers often pressure us to buy the merchandise. It's offered to employees at a discounted rate, but still feels like a scam.

In reality, we're heavily encouraged to buy their merchandise. to imitate for the season. Winter's look is dark denim jeans, black converse shoes, and a plaid shirt. Our choice in colors for the shirt come in a variety, but I don't like any of the patterns, so I choose to wear the crisp white shirt we were allowed to wear in Fall. So, far I've gotten away with it. It was raining out, so I grabbed my favorite black double-breasted jacket and the umbrella I bought the other day. It was all black with a pine wood handle. While I was halfway through my shift I got a text from Alessandra. *We need to talk, call me when you can.* I knew something had happened, but I had no way of knowing what. Since I was still at work, I dismissed it for the time being. Once I was finally off, I called her back. When she answered I could hear the nervousness in her voice. I asked her what was wrong, and she informed me that she was worried people were starting to talk about us. I asked what she meant, and she said, "you know, what we've done." Naturally, my next question was what made her think that. She said that one of our mutual friends made a joke about oral sex to her and it seemed directed at her. I paused.

"Which friend?" I asked.

"That's not important," she answered.

"If you're calling me about it, it is important."

"Who knows?"

"Who knows what?"

"Who knows what happened between us?"

"As far as I know, the only people that know are you, Evan, Tiffany and I." That was a lie. In addition to Will, I'd told Leo and Ezra one time while we were stoned at The Village. The Village by the way is Villa Valle's most popular (and only) outdoor mall. It's full of cafés, shops, and restaurants and we like to go there stoned because a) it has food and b) we can just blend in, and people watch.

Anyway, I lied because I thought it would stop things from escalating. In hindsight it wasn't the best decision I ever made, but at the time it seemed like a sound one. Besides, I knew Will would never tell anyone, neither would Leo and Ezra. They certainly wouldn't ever make jokes to Alessandra about it. We had all known each other's personal business for years and never spread any of it. That meant it had to be Tiffany who gossiped about us, but Alessandra would never believe that or perhaps it was just paranoia on Alessandra's part. Perhaps someone else knew. But who else could know? We were at The Village when I told Leo and Ezra, maybe someone overheard. All these thoughts raced through my head.

"I'm probably just being paranoid then," she said.

My nerves settled again. "Try not to worry about it, and sorry you had to hear anything," I said. Right after I hung up, I sent a message to Ezra and Leo asking them not to make any crude jokes when Alessandra is around, just for safe measure.
Leo responded first with a no problem. Unfortunately, Ezra opened his message on his laptop a couple days later, while seated at a café at The Village. He stepped away from the computer to use the restroom and asked Leo to watch it.

Unfortunately, Ramsey Wallace and few of his friends walked up to where Ezra had been seated. Now Ramsey is smart, charming, and very entertaining, but he can also be quite intrusive at times. And when he learns something that he can hold over someone's head, he turns into the most obnoxious person you'll ever meet. The way I heard the story, Ramsey and Leo exchanged hellos and then Ramsey in his typical curious way asked what Ezra had been looking at on the laptop. Leo made it seem like nothing interesting, but Ramsey didn't buy that. He darted around the table to see for himself and before Leo could stop him Ramsey had read half of my message to Ezra out loud.

By the time he finished everyone except for Leo was in shock. Very few ever got to see the side of her that I did. Though the message did not go into any detail about what happened with us, the fact that I sent it implied the obvious, Alessandra and I had hooked up. As Leo went on to tell me, things got a lot worse. Apparently, Alessandra showed up to The Village because she had planned on meeting Ramsey there. Ramsey read the message aloud a second time, just as Ezra was returning. Ezra embarrassed closed his laptop. Alessandra was mortified. A few hours later, I received a cryptic text that read, "how could you do it?" from Ramsey. Utterly confused, I called him to ask exactly what it was I'd done.

"You really don't know?" he said.

"No, please enlighten me," I said.

"You took advantage of an innocent girl."

"What? I did no such thing!"

"Oh, come on. We all know you got oral from Alessandra. She told me she had just broken up with her boyfriend and you took advantage of her in a weak moment."

I was red hot with rage. I couldn't believe what I was hearing. I had never expected to have to explain myself to anyone about this, but I wasn't going to let Alessandra skew the circumstances to make me out to be the bad guy. "Really? Funny because we hooked up before she broke up with her boyfriend as well as after. I have a barrage of texts to prove that she, not I instigated this whole affair."

"Oh. Sorry," he said.

"It's alright man, I could see why you'd think that. But that's not me."

"I know, I kind of thought that the whole time, but she was so convincing and the message..."

That's how I learned that Ramsey had read the message I sent to Ezra on Ezra's open laptop. I was horrified. I was all for sexual liberation and being honest about my experiences, but I genuinely respected the fact that Alessandra wasn't. I'd been foolish to tell more than one person about us and expect it not to get out. Villa Valle is a small town after all, and secrets don't stay buried for long in small towns.

"I've got to go man, but I would never prey on anyone's emotions like that."

"I figured," he said.

"Anyway, Alessandra and I are finished."

"Same here." With that I hung up and the next number I dialed was Alessandra's. I asked her to meet me at Montclair Park to talk. She agreed. As soon as she arrived, I approached her, calm, and cold.

"Alright let's make this quick."

"What?" she asked.

"You could have irrevocably ruined my name and my friendship with Ramsey, for what; to save your reputation as some paragon of purity? You failed, I know everything and it's over."

"Ok, hold on, I never meant to..." she started.

"I don't even care what your excuses are. This pathetic charade ends now."

"I just wanted..."

"I don't care. You know what? I lied. I lied to you when I said I hadn't told anyone. I told a few friends in confidence. But I sent that message to try to make up for it, to try to defend you. I don't even know why I did though, because you readily threw me under the bus." I proceeded to tell her that I don't want to see her anymore, not as lovers, not as friends, not even around town. "If I run into you and you so much as make eye contact with me, I'll forward every single dirty text message you ever sent me to everyone we know. Understood?" It was an empty threat, but I knew it would work. I couldn't follow through with it even if I'd wanted to. I had already deleted all except the very recent messages she had sent me, but she wasn't aware of that. I was over and that was all that mattered.

"Yes," she said. She sounded stunned. If I were her, I too would have been completely taken aback. She'd never seen my dark side before, if you could call it that.

"Cool. Well, have a nice life and stay out of mine." I walked away a wreck. Our interaction made all of the muscles in my body tense up. I felt betrayed and justified, yet I hated being so cruel to someone I had once been so tender to.

December 30, 2009

This past week I was questioned regarding the Alessandra fiasco as I had expected. However, it wasn't as frequent or high in volume as these things usually are due to Christmas. Thank God for Christmas! Everyone was too busy going on vacation or beaming about what gifts they received to focus on me. Luckily, with Kate and Parker still away I didn't have endure one of Kate's forced family celebrations. Instead, I went to the Perrins for Christmas dinner (since Mr. & Mrs. Perrin insisted), then raced home to eat popcorn and watch television. Believe it or not I rarely really watch television. I guess that's because I'm rarely ever home.

Anyhow I saw Lexie today. Seeing her always does a world of good for me. We caught up and laughed about the Alessandra situation, then I went home again. As I reached the building, I got a phone call from an old classmate, Lara. Lara was an aspiring make-up artist and stylist who I met in junior high. I think the last time I saw her was her sweet sixteen. Her parents rented a stretch Hummer limousine for the evening. Lara picked a handful of friends, the limo collected each of us, and chauffeured us to dinner at Katsuya. I guess she must have saved my number. The favor she needed was for me to model for her tomorrow. It's the perfect distraction from my present drama, so I agreed.

December 31, 2009

I awoke at 6:00 am, dressed and arrived at the Bebe Howard School in Woodland Hills by 9:00 am. Bebe Howard was a well-connected Hollywood photographer. She runs the cosmetology school Lara attends. The building was well lit and extremely tidy. The other models were posing in front of the mirrors set about adjusting their clothes. I mentioned to Lara that it seemed a little odd to do anything on New Year's Eve.

"Bebe doesn't care what day it is. The industry doesn't take breaks, and neither should we," Lara said. "She's a bit demanding, but it's only because she has high standards. She's worked with the most glamorous people."

Just then Bebe entered the room. I wasn't sure how much of the conversation she'd heard, but she joined in. "They were only glamorous because I knew how to make them that way," Bebe said in a heavy transatlantic accent. She was a relic of Old Hollywood alright.

By 10:00 am it was my turn. I was dressed in a neat cream cardigan, black shirt and crisp blue jeans that I bought from Pulse. Bebe snapped several shots of me from the front, side profile, and seated. She made me lift my chin, tilt my head, tuck my hands in and out of his pockets, which all seemed very awkward but looked nice when she showed me the still on her camera. About an hour and a half and three touch-ups later, we had finished. Bebe complemented Lara's work as well as my performance.

"You should really look into doing this professionally darling," she said. I laughed, thanked her, and left. When I got home, I noticed luggage spread about the living room. *Kate must be home,* I thought. *Oh well, tonight is New Year's Eve and I'm not letting her ruin my plans.* I showered, got dressed, and went out into the night. With me were Will and Troy Sanz, whom Will and I were finally able to convince to come out with us. We cruised down to the Sunset Strip at around 9:30 pm to eat at Carney's Diner. If you've never been to Carney's you should go, it's a diner set up inside of preserved old train car that sits on actual tracks.

We ordered chili dogs and cheese fries. Greasy foods to help us absorb the alcohol we planned to consume that night. At around 10:00 pm our plan went into motion. We left Carney's and Will drove his us in his Camry down to a little liquor store Hollywood Boulevard. We purchased a handle of Captain Morgan's coconut rum, drove to a secluded spot on a little residential street nearby and took turns taking sips until we were drunk enough to feel it, but not too drunk to walk. This was a huge thrill for Troy, who kept mentioning what an adventure we were having.

Will and I just laughed, feeling appreciated, and we all walked down the boulevard to The Ruby, the same club I had gone to with Tyson Montes a few months ago. We reached the front steps and put on our best sober acts so we could make it past club security. Luckily for us we didn't have to wait in line long since I reserved spots for us in November. Once inside the first thing we noticed was how packed the main room was. It was the same in the two other rooms, which was expected since it was New Year's Eve. We danced around until 11:45, that's when we decided to venture onto the stage.

At 11:55 pm the room was filled with anticipation. The various TV screens mounted on the walls stopped playing music videos and aired a not so live countdown of the ball dropping in New York City. It was just us, an amazing DJ, a room full of people, and Dick Clark. As the clock struck 11:59 the whole club got giddy and started to shout. Will, Troy, and I stood close to each other with our arms around each other's shoulder. The year began to flash before my eyes. I saw myself confronting Leona, the drama with Alessandra, the mistakes with Chloe and Kasey. I thought about school and fighting with Kate. The countdown began and everyone around us began shouting *ten, nine*. This year had been rough. I couldn't believe I'd survived it – *seven, six*. I was determined to make this year different, *four, three*. No, this year was going to be different! *One...*

January 3, 2010

It's been three days since the New Year began. I've been trying to be a better person, but that's easier said than done. School is boring me to death, but I've put all my focus into it. I've been attending all my classes and working hard on assignments. I really want to get the hell out of Villa Community College and transfer into a university as soon as possible. I desperately need a change of scenery. I've spent too much time here.

Today is proving especially difficult, as it's Leona's birthday. I told myself I'd let go and move on. Yet, I can't help but think about what we were doing this time last year. We were strolling hand in hand down the Santa Monica Pier. It was strange because we hadn't held hands before then. We were holding each other close at a café. We were laughing and not thinking about anything too serious. I was falling in love. God only knows what she was thinking. I told myself I wouldn't focus on that, but it's really hard not to.

Fuck I hate today. Maybe I'll always hate it. Maybe I'll never get over her, no matter whom I end up with, if I end up with anyone at all. Maybe I'll write poetry and songs about her and go crazy until I die. Probably not though. I know I'm young and I'll meet someone else. I know these years are just the foundation meant to be built upon by other experiences. But none of that helps. None of that makes it hurt any less. I wish it didn't hurt at all. I wish I didn't feel anything at all. I realize it's not even her fault. It's my fault. She may have been misleading in the beginning, but there was a point where she was honest. I just didn't take it well.

I should have gotten over her, just as she suggested. Instead, I continued to go over there. I continued to allow myself to have hope for something that was never going to happen. That was all me. The remnants of the idealistic, idiotic, bastard I used to be still lives on inside of me. It appears only in glimpses now, with Duncan and Gisele, but I'm sick of it. I've been trying to kill that fantasy-prone romantic inside of me for the longest. Tonight, I came one step closer.

Tonight, on Leona's special day. I went to Psychobabble Café in Los Feliz

Village. I found a petite artist girl there. She had a septum ring, and both her ears were pierced from the tip to the lobe. She wore thick framed glasses and had dark hair with purple streaks in it, which she pulled back into a ponytail. She spoke confidently as she sipped her iced mocha. We talked about The Doors, since "LA Woman" happened to be playing in the café. Her name was Ilene ...or Irene, I can't recall. The important part is I went back to her place and fucked her. Excuse my language, but that's the only way I can describe it. It wasn't intimate. It wasn't lovemaking. We did not get closer. We did not learn anything about each other. We walked into her studio, had a silly little conversation about the furniture, and then we started kissing. We kissed harder and harder as she led me to her bed not but a few feet away.

The covers were crimson. I noticed though we never got under them. We were too busy tearing each other's clothes off. Call it sublimation, escapism, artistic expression – call it whatever the hell you want. Once we hit her mattress things really started up. No time was wasted. Before I knew it, we were grinding our bodies into one another. We were thrusting, writhing, biting, and gripping at each other's bare flesh for leverage. The goal was to keep going until all the anguish in me dissipated. I wanted nothing more than to remain lost in the throes of passion forever. Unfortunately, like all good things, my hookup with the artist came to an end. I was elated after we both finished, but that post-sex euphoria was fleeting. It didn't take long before desire returned to consume me.

January 16, 2010

A couple of my old mistakes have come back to haunt me. The first involves Chloe. Apparently, she told everyone at VVHS that we had oral sex. I learned this from Parker's best friend and band mate Brian's girlfriend. Complicated, I know, but it came up one-night last week while we were all getting stoned in Brian's room. I decided to tell everyone the truth, that we didn't. I was going to forget it and move on, but then I realized it bothered the hell out of me. This was supposed to be a new year and here I was being weighed down by the same old shit.

Instead of discussing the issue like a mature young adult, I resorted to my old familiar behavior and lashed out at Kasey. Drama ensued. At the time I felt justified. The whole situation in Chloe's garage seemed like a set up from the beginning. I wondered how someone who was supposed to be my friend, could let me walk into a trap. I wondered why Kasey didn't seem to be troubled by it at all. I told him exactly how I felt.

"You just stood by and watched it all," I said accusingly. I was irritated, but I also felt manipulated and betrayed. It was ironic after all the games I played myself last year.

"What was I supposed to do Colin?" he asked.

"I don't know. How about be a good friend?" I said. It was an unfair jab. His loyalty was rightfully where it should have been, with Chloe. He was far closer to her than me. She was one of his best friends after all.

"You've stretched that card way too thin," he said. It took me by surprise. I wasn't expecting a rebuttal from him. He had always been so amiable, but everyone has their limits.

"What's that supposed to mean?" I said. I had grown beyond irritated.

"It means I've done nothing but be a good friend, even though you totally screwed with my head," Kasey said. He wasn't going to lie down and take it. I was picking a fight, but he was ready for it.

"I never meant to mislead you," I said. I had to stop and take a mental step back. I hadn't instigated all of this, but I had been totally complicit. Before I could finish explaining, Kasey cut me off.

"Don't even say it," he said. "Maybe it's time you started taking responsibility for your actions instead of hiding behind circumstance and good intentions." That stung, probably because it was true. I knew it right after he said it, but I was Kate's child. I wasn't going to let him win. I had to hurt him back.

"Honestly dude, go fuck yourself. No one else will," I said, then I hung up. It was terribly cruel. I've come to recognize that I'm both the hero and the villain of my story. Maybe Kasey was just trying to be a good friend to Chloe by helping her get what she wanted. Maybe I was just shifting my own guilt onto him so I could cope. Regardless, I decided it was best to distance myself from Kasey and his friends.

The second mistake involves one of Leona's friends. Her name is Stella and it's not what you think. Well not quite. I met Stella in August. She was dating a friend of mine (and I use the term friend very loosely) named Jeff. During the course of their relationship Jeff and Stella propositioned me for a three-way. They even took me to a 'let's-have- a-threesome-lunch.' No, I'm not kidding you. I didn't know what to say, for the first time ever as Kate might point out, so I just made a joke. I asked if I could think about it and of course they said yes. That wasn't the only time they ever brought it up either. Each time I was forced to come up with some kind of excuse as to avoid saying no and hurting their feelings or worse, sparking an argument. They aren't the kind of people who take rejection well. I mean they were pretty sure of themselves.

If I had just said 'sorry Jeff, I don't want to double-team your girlfriend with you' I would certainly been asked why. I find having to explain myself in situation like that is loads more difficult to deal with than anything. So, instead I invented doctor appointments, study groups, work schedules that were impossible to get around - something new each time they asked.

Two weeks ago, they broke up. It was a Tuesday. I know this because it was just two days after their breakup, that I found out from Lexie that Jeff hit on her.

When I confronted Jeff, he lied about it. Maybe this happened to teach me a lesson about my own lies, maybe not. Given the history I've shared with you about my high school best friend, you could probably predict how I reacted. I was livid. I don't exactly know why I was so upset now think about it. Maybe it's a guy thing to be territorial. Maybe it was just the lying part or maybe it's because I didn't end up with Lexie. She was undiscoverable to me and here he was trying to discover her behind my back. Maybe I was just being shallow, or maybe it was because of all the shit I shared with him about the way I used to feel about her.

Whatever it was, I was enraged. What made it worse was he had just recently asked me if I still had feelings for Lexie. What made it worse was when I gave an inconclusive answer, he said I should go for it again and I seemed better matched with her than with Leona. When I read the texts Lexie forwarded me, he finally admitted it. His defense was that he was being stupid and that I was one of his closest friends. Stella had been texting me every day since they broke up, because I guess she felt like I was a good shoulder to lean on. I understood everything with Jeff. Anyway, three days ago Stella told me a bunch of stuff about how Jeff said he still cares for her and how she just knew they were going to get back together. I immediately felt conflicted. I felt like she deserved to know what an ass Jeff was. He was two-timing her or attempting to anyway. I felt like she deserved to know about all the times he told me he was just with her for the sex. But if I ratted him out, I wouldn't be any better in the situation, would I?

Here's where the mistake comes in and this one's a double-whammy. I went to the one person I believed could help me sort it out. I shouldn't have, but I felt like I had to. I went to Leona. She let me in and was both surprised and oddly happy to see me. On the way from her front door to her living room, I started ranting about Jeff and Stella. Leona insisted that I had to tell Stella everything. She told me about how Stella was considering marrying Jeff before they broke up.

She further shared how Jeff hit on her too. He started around the time we fell apart. Around the time she told me to get over it. I didn't tell him about that, but I did tell him I was really disappointed things hadn't worked out with Leona. He told me he was too and that he had been rooting for us. Suddenly, revenge was the only thing I could think of. Out of a mixture of a desire for retribution and actual concern for Stella, I told her about Jeff. Of course she didn't believe me. *Jeff would never say those things about her. Jeff loved her. Jeff didn't care about Lexie or Leona. He was just flirting. Jeff was her soulmate, and I was just jealous. Blah blah blah.* It was nauseating. Leona called Stella a stupid bitch. We laughed about it together and she made us something to eat. I stayed there for hours. We talked and mocked Jeff and Stella. It was just like old times.

February 11, 2010

School's back in session and I've been spending far too much time with Leona since the Jeff and Stella debacle. I've been going over her house after classes. I catch myself laughing too hard, smiling too wide, but I can't help it. She seems to have changed. Maybe now that she's a year older, things could really be different between the two of us, maybe not. She's throwing out a lot of signs though. She jokes about how perfect we are for each other. She's joked about that kind of thing before, so I try not to pay too much attention to it. I noticed she's been talking about the long-term a lot more as well. She's mentioned running away together and getting married. How we can finally get away from our crazy families. I haven't told her about Ilene, or Irene, or whatever her name was. I feel a bit guilty, but we'll cross that bridge when we come to it.

When she says things like that my blood runs cold. I have all these memories of the way things were prior to our big fall out and of course the way I felt afterwards. I remember the ire that seeped into me and the bile that churned in my stomach. I hated her so much, because I'd loved her so much. I try to ignore all of that now. I try to just be in the moment and be her friend. It's beyond difficult though. We spend a ridiculous amount of time doing couple-like things together. She'll walk me to work. I'll wait for her after her classes. We'll eat lunch together and she's even invited me over for dinner. We spend hours lying in her bed together just talking about stuff. Sometimes I feel like she's waiting for me to make a move, but our past leaves me too uncertain to take the chance. Besides, I'd hate to ruin the intimacy we're establishing with sex. I don't know what the hell I'm letting happen here, but I don't want to figure it all out either. As Oscar Wilde once wrote, a burnt child loves the fire.

February 27, 2010

It happened. I finally cracked. I'd been avoiding Leona after my last entry. I realized I was slipping into old, unhealthy, patterns. It was so easy to slip with her. I really thought she'd changed. I thought there was a possibility of a chance for us, but as usual I was dead wrong. Look at me, I sound pathetic. Anyway, during the course of the past week she called and sent text messages, but I rarely answered. On the occasions where I did, I made it a point to be vague and aloof. Vague about the next time I'll see her, aloof when she wants to discuss something personal. I'm tired of being her therapist. I'm tired of being her crutch.

She's using me to be everything, but what I'd like us to be. I'm disgracing myself by carrying on with her. Dishonoring the painful experiences from our not-too-distant past that I thought I'd learned from. I realized all of this and so I decided to push her away. I was doing so well, until I ran into her on Thursday. It had just finished raining. I was done with my classes for the day, so I went to Montclair Park to take a walk and relax. I was heading out of the main passageway when we saw each other.

"Colin!" she said excitedly. "Where have you been?"

"I've been busy," I said keeping to my promise to myself. Vague and aloof.

"I bet, balancing school and work must be hectic. I honestly don't know how you do it. Are you still taking that human sexuality class? I think I might take that next fall." Leona always spoke a mile a minute. It seemed like she never paused to breathe. Most times, I found it endearing. I knew I could take a break from leading the conversation when I was with her. She was social enough for the both of us. For some reason though, I didn't find her blathering endearing that day. I didn't want to stand there listening to her go on and on about the minutia of our lives. She stopped herself and as if she read my thoughts, she said, "I'm probably boring you."

"No, you're not," I said. I was lying through my teeth.

"You don't have to lie," she said. "Anyway, why haven't I seen you?"

That was a question I hadn't been expecting. I fumbled. "What do you mean?

We just went over the fact that I've been busy..."

"Yeah, but that's surface bullshit," she replied cutting me off. "I was going along with it, rambling, and hoping you'd stop me to tell me the truth. Instead, you waited for me to cut myself off, which is very difficult to do mind you." She had a way of saying things, even things that were serious with a light-hearted flare.

"There isn't any deeper truth to be found," I lied again.

"Really?" she demanded.

I thought back to the reason I had begun avoiding her. Like I said I'd started to slip. I'd started to fall for the idea of being with her again. Then one night I went over for television and chips. It was already late so Leona suggested I sleep over. She lives with just her mother and Ms. Cavanaugh is used to me being there all the time, so I agreed. She set everything up in her room. "Come sleep next to me," she said. I shouldn't have, but I agreed. We were lying there together recalling memories from summer.

"Remember those parties in your room." she said.

"God yes, there was Shisha everywhere!" I replied.

"It was embedded in the carpet. Along with coal stains! I can only imagine how your mom must have flipped."

"She hated it! But she kept saying it was okay to invite you guys." She laughed and rolled around. She was in her pajamas, and I was clad in a t-shirt and some old shorts her cousin left there a while ago.

"I washed them. I tried to return them to him, but he said he didn't need them," she informed me. There we were in bed together having the time of our lives. I was lying on my back and she on her side facing me. I'd look over at her every now and then, when she'd make one of her famous comedic ludicrous statements and she'd say "what?" and I'd just laugh. It went like this way for a while, then she did what she always does. She probably doesn't even know she's doing, but she *always* does it. She killed the moment. She blurted out that she hadn't had sex in days. "I better call Cale," she said.

Cale is her sex buddy's name. And yes, his name is just Cale. It's not short for

Caleb or anything, just Cale. What kind of a fucking name is that? It sounds like a disorder. I've got a bad case of Cale. The doctors say they don't know what to do about it. I took a silent breath, looked her right in the eyes and said the following:

"You haven't seen me because I'm recovering. Recovering from my god-awful addiction to you." I thought I was over it. I mean this time was supposed to be different. This time I wasn't going to let her slip into my heart. This time I had plans to be cold and unruly. Yet as I laid beside her, as we smiled and laughed right before sleep caught up with us and dragged us off to dreaming; I knew this time was going to end up just like every other time. She'd permeate my waking thoughts, then seep into my unconscious and make a home there. She'd get me to go everywhere and anywhere with her.

I'd do anything she'd asked me to. She'd be kind, sweet, and misleading. She'd invite me to witness her most private moments, then you'd pretend it was all meaningless. I knew what lay ahead. When she proved me right two weeks ago, I thought *this is it, so long goodnight to all my strength*. But the strangest thing happened, I didn't bend at her pulsing words. I didn't break. I didn't shatter. Her descriptions of her lover flew right above my head. I laughed at the predictability of it all. I could have cried, but I laughed instead. I knew in that moment that I could survive her.

She paused and looked down at her shoes. "Oh, all right."
I'm glad never told her about sleeping with what's her face. She didn't deserve to know anyway.

March 14, 2010

I've forgotten all about Leona. I'm already onto my next mistake. Her name is Gisele. Gisele is 5'3", with dark wavy hair, a thick figure, and a nice ass. She's a party girl by all accounts and a senior at Harry S. Truman High. I like being with her because I feel like I can be myself around her. So, we've been hooking up since we met. Honestly, it's refreshing to be back in the game. Not to put anything on the line. Up until recently it was nothing special, nothing serious. One of us would go to a party, ask if the other was going to be there, we'd meet up and fool around.

Kate even let me borrow her car a few times. It feels weird to call Kate that, *Mom*, but things have been better between us ever since she's returned from Seattle. Back to the story though, I like Gisele. I like the way she comes over to the apartment to get ready before we go out. She never has much to do. She applies a little makeup here, changes into a dress or just changes shoes; no matter what she always does it here and I like that. We share my bathroom. I zip or button her up when I need to. She always either fixes my collar or smoothens out one of my cardigans for me. It's cheesy but it's sweet. It bonds us. But we're just having fun. It's nothing serious.

April 4, 2010

Gisele and I have been texting each other more often. We joke at each other's expenses. We kiss each other like we mean it. It's kind of nice and a tad bit more serious, I guess. Here's the thing though, I don't want to get too heavily involved with her. Can you blame me? I have more than enough reason for my faith in people to be shaken. I don't know if I can believe in anyone who's attracted to me. I certainly don't think I can be in a relationship again. But you never know. I guess I have to wait and see how things play out. I'd like her to stick around, that much I know. I enjoy her company and Kate *hates* her, which is always an added bonus. Kate and I are hardly speaking these days by the way. I don't know what it is with that woman and having to control everything.

April 13, 2010

I'm now officially dating Gisele. I was conflicted about saying yes at first. She's 18 and out of high school. I told myself no more high school girls after Chloe. There's something about Gisele that makes it hard for me to resist. She kind of has a bad reputation and I'm into it. I'm not interested in only having sex with her. Honest. She intrigues me. She surprised me by asking me out instead of it being the other way around. She's a go-getter. Sure, I could see the way things were going. I could sense that we were getting closer and closer, but there was still so much in between us. I did not expect to end up with her, especially not after I found out she slept with Brian.

Yes, this is the same Brian that is in my brother Parker's band. I guess this happened when he first came back from Juilliard last summer. This is before she and I knew each other, so it doesn't even matter. The only thing that's irritating is I learned of it from Brian and Brian is the kind of guy who's far too proud of whom he's slept with. Despite all of this, I still gave in and said yes. I must admit I've wanted this kind of companionship for a while.

She not a substitute for anything or ego filler the way Alessandra was. Being with her doesn't feel like a perilous regret the way Chloe did. Gisele is different. I don't even care that Kate hates her anymore. There is a slight hitch to this situation though. She suggested we make it an open relationship. I actually really like this idea. It feels safe. Like I said I really can't imagine giving so much of myself to someone again and this way I don't have to. We agreed to two rules. The first is 'don't ask, don't tell.' That means, we won't share information about pursuits with each other, unless it'll put the other's health in jeopardy (i.e., contracting an STD). The second rule is friends and family are off limits. Seems simple enough.

April 19, 2010

Gisele's been sending me texts daily and I'm beyond irritated about it. It's not the frequency of the texts that bothers me, it's the content. She's literally sends me pictures of her lunch. When I'm not receiving lovely photographs of what she's eating, she's babbling on about some irrelevant subject or another. She lacks depth. I want depth! On top of that the more and more we communicate, the more I'm starting to believe she's just using the open relationship idea to segue into having a committed relationship and I don't like being manipulated that way.

If she wanted a monogamous relationship she should have just asked. I've either spoken to or texted nearly her every night since last week. On the nights we're not together, she tries to advocate for me to hook up with other girls. It doesn't come across as genuine though. It feels hollow. Her mouth says 'go and have fun' but the undercurrent is 'I'm technically your girlfriend. If you sleep with someone else, I'm going to be really upset, but this is me pretending not to care.' That irritates me more than getting pictures of her food. I don't know what to do about it though. I like her. We're not having sex, and I still like her. I've had sex with other girls, and I still like her.

Whether I'm hovering sweaty and breathless over a cute bookstore clerk, lying in bed with a Canadian exchange student, or going down on the goth girl I met at art walk; I still want to be with Gisele. I feel guilty when Gisele calls just to hear my voice, but we made a rule. I'm just following the rules. I know it's stupid. I know what she really wants. I'd give up all the screwing around for her, cause I mean aside from this stuff there really isn't anything wrong with our 'relationship,' but I don't know. It's difficult. I need to know she wants it. I recently found out she can't even tell her parents she's dating me. I knew this might be a problem.

After all, she is still in high school and that's why I decided not to push the sex issue, but I don't think I can go on banging other girls when she's all I really want. Maybe I'm expecting too much for her to make the first move in solidifying things, but

I have my reasons. The bile still churns in my stomach. Bitterness still pumps through my veins from the last time I let someone in. It's still too soon to open up again/ I'd rather be heartless and cruel. I'd rather drown my sorrows in other girls. Call me an asshole, but I'll do whatever it takes to protect myself.

April 27, 2010

It's over between Gisele and me. Last weekend I discovered that she slept with pretty much all of her close guy friends. I try to avoid slut-shaming as a rule. I'm not innocent myself, but this revelation was intensely uncomfortable for me. It all came to a head while we were at one of her friend's house parties. It happened before we started seeing each other. We're not even that serious of a relationship, but I would have liked a heads up. I'd give her a heads up if we were in the same vicinity as any of the girls I'd slept with. *What the hell is wrong with her? First the Brian thing and now this.*

I was in the line for the bathroom at the party and a guy she'd introduced as a "long time friend" started talking to me. Then he just blurts out that they slept together last summer. The same summer during which she slept with Brian. Now, I'm no saint and everyone has a past, but she should have really told me this. I've seen this guy more than a handful of times. It makes me wonder if they're still sleeping together. I wonder if every time he sees me, he's thinking this guy is a fucking idiot.

Here's the cherry on top, he goes on to tell me about the other five guys she slept with that same summer. All five of these guys just happen to be at the party, hanging out together. I asked Gisele about it. She confirmed it was true and I ended it right then and there. It was humiliating to be put in that situation. I know she didn't mean for it to happen that way, but it doesn't change anything. I felt like the drama would only continue unless I ended it. I mean if someone doesn't have the foresight to warn you that you're going to be surrounded by five different people they've banged over the course of a three-month break, then it can't work.

May 8, 2010

Brian invited me to his party. At first, I wasn't going to go. Everyone was guaranteed to be a at least three years younger than me. As I was leaving work, I decided there would be no harm in showing up for a little while. Besides, Brian is cool, and I knew Parker would be there. Parker seemed really excited I said I mentioned going earlier today. When I got home from work, I showered and changed into a thin black cardigan, a plain white shirt, and slim black jeans. To no one's surprise Kate refused to let me take the car. She walked out into the living room.

"Let me guess, you're going out," she said sarcastically.

"Would you rather me stay here and exchange pleasantries with you all night?" I asked just as sarcastically. I was always good at playing Kate's little games with her.

"No, go out and have a grand time," she said. That was unexpected. What was this some sort of attempt at reverse psychology? I did not know how to respond. I tried to think of something witty to say but only managed to say thanks.

"You're welcome. You look nice by the way." Again, thoroughly unexpected.

"Thanks..."

"Only I do wish you'd stand up straight."

There is the criticism I knew had to be lurking just around the corner. If It feels too good to be true with her, it usually is. Worst part is I thought I was standing up straight.

"Gee, thanks Mom."

"When you get back you should brainstorm on some productive things to do."

I guess going to school full-time and working part-time isn't productive enough for her. Sure, I like to party, but Kate only sees a glimpse of that. Anything she surmises further about me is an uneducated guess. I brushed off the slicing comments and stepped into a comfortable pair of black tennis shoes. Mere minutes later I had boarded bus that dropped me off three blocks from Brian's house. I walked the rest of the way. When I arrived, it took me a moment to remember which house was Brian's.

Though I soon recognized the electric blue front door. Even in the dark, that blue door contrasted smoothly against the hazel walls of the rest of the outside of his two-story home. I walked up the pathway, gave a few quick loud knocks and within minutes Brian's girlfriend answered the door. I can never remember her name and it doesn't really matter because none of Brian's girlfriends ever last too long anyway.

As I was ushered into the living room I spotted Parker. He walked up to me, gave me a brief hug then introduced me to a few of his friends. In the dim lit that emitted from the chandelier above us and a tall silver lamp in the corner of the room. I could see teenage bodies everywhere. It was the typical high school crowd. The girls all painted faces, tight fitting outfits, and high heels and the boys in casual wear that they probably found at Gap. It brought me back to my years at VVHS.

Anyway, I maneuvered around the neat black and white matching furniture to the kitchen where Parker and I both grabbed beers. I then made my way to the smaller of two large black sofas and sat down next to a guy who seemed friendly enough. Parker had disappeared at this point, so I decided to make friends. I started talking to the seemingly friendly guy seated next to me and learned his name was named Jack. Jack is thin, of medium height, with dark hair, light brown eyes, and a facial structure eerily resembling that of James Dean. He even has the same kind of haircut, although he put no effort into making it a pompadour. This is why his friends sometimes call him Jimmy. Oh, and I also learned that his name is just Jack, it's not short for John or anything.

While we were talking, two guys from the opposite end of the room came over to say hi. Their names were Ethan and Immanuel. Ethan, like Jack and my brother, is a senior at VVHS. Immanuel is 19, a year younger than me. He graduated from Truman. Ethan's known Brian since their freshman year. Immanuel met the group a few months ago.

"Glad to see people actually socializing," Ethan said.

"Glad I met Colin. This party was quickly becoming a bore," Jack said.

"Why is everyone so closed off?" asked Immanuel.

I thought about my own situation and laughed. "Cause the world is vile."

"It's a party. We're supposed to check our cynicism at the door," Jack said. We all laughed. We split up and reconvened several times during the night. By the end of the party, almost everyone in attendance was either too drunk or stoned to drive home, so we all slept over. In the morning, I exchanged numbers with a few people, including my newfound friends, and left.

May 19, 2010

Jack, Ethan, Immanuel and I have hung out a lot more. I found out Ethan's gay, Jack is insomniac, and Immanuel has the habit of spreading himself too thin. They're a good group of guys. I decided to rent a motel room and throw a little party last weekend, because why the hell not? There were 4 girls there in addition to the guys: Holly, Quinn, and the inseparable Nilsson cousins. It was supposed to be small, but within an hour we had more 25-30 people in the room. Everyone was dancing, laughing, and drinking. I decided to try MDMA for the first time because Jack had some, and why the hell not?

I didn't feel anything different for a good thirty minutes, then all of a sudden, the music playing in the background began to fill me. Everything felt beautiful and limitless. I smoked a cigarette Troy lit for me and all I swear after I finished it all I wanted to do was smoke a thousand more. We'd bought about 6 cases of beer and hard liquor all over the place. There was vodka, rum, tequila, and my favorite, gin. I hardly touched any of it. I felt too good. The room felt like sky. My fingers tingled anytime I touched anything. My spine shivered anytime anyone in the room touched me. Everything felt amazing. *Amazing.* That's all I could say whenever anyone asked me how I felt or what something was like. The guys were joking about how crazy I had gotten once the e had kicked in.

"Bet you wouldn't kiss Ethan," Jack said.

"Are you kidding me? I'm Colin fucking Prescott." I said. Now I try to be modest, but over the years I have realized that I'm gifted in certain areas. I'm fairly intelligent, fairly handsome, and extremely social. I've learned in critical moments to use these talents to get what I want. Like everything else in life there's no guarantee. Things can get out of control and slip through my fingers just like everyone else. I mean I'm only human. But when I'm on a substance, I feel different. I feel more in touch with that inner self. That self I try to keep tame and modest in all other aspects of my life. I think we all feel that way, that's why we take drugs. It's a temporary escape.

Don't get me wrong, I know I'm pretty lucky to be who I am and to have the opportunities I've had in life.

But when I'm under the influence, it feels like I'm much more aligned with my true self. It's more than casual confidence or slight arrogance. It's heightened awareness unparalleled. So, there I was, Mr. Popularity already, on molly, and feeling like I own the world. My friends were daring me to do something they thought was wild, but little did they know I've already done before. I beckoned Ethan over and kissed him right on the mouth. The music pounded out of the stereo.

Holly watched intently. She walked over and grabbed me around my waist. "That looks hot," she said impishly. "I want some." I kissed her passionately, and then kissed Ethan matching the intensity. I went back and forth between the two for several minutes, as a relatively shocked Jack and Immanuel looked on. Holly, Ethan, and I finished with a three-way kiss, and then we stopped fooling around to rejoin the party. By 2:00 am we were all worn out. The girls had left. We cleaned up as much as we could and went to sleep. I just got home from it all. It was an epic night.

June 10, 2010

The guys and I have grown pretty tight. I've gotten a chance to see just what kind, caring, people they really are, and I know how rare that is. They're all more loyal and trustworthy than anyone I ever knew. Jack, though impatient and feverishly addicted to risking trouble, loves to hug everyone, and was infinitely generous. He'd stand up for you in a heartbeat, no matter the circumstance. Immanuel always picks up when you call, no matter what time it is, and he'd be there in a flash if you needed him. Ethan, the baby of the group, needs a little more care than he could give at times, but he always listens and tells you exactly what he thinks- no sugar coating. I really appreciate having these people in my life. They feel more like family than friends. They're not perfect and neither am I. It just fits.

Immanuel and I went to the annual car show on Grant Boulevard. We found a booth selling beer and since he had a fake ID, he was able to buy some for us. I always wanted a fake, but never knew exactly how to get one. I suppose I never really needed one, alcohol was everywhere. It was easy enough to get away with drinking at the car show too. The streets were so crowded that the cops couldn't even chase you even if they wanted to. Once we were good and drunk, we decided to take the train to Hollywood.

We were completely composed leaving Villa Valle but for some reason once we got to our destination we lost all sense. We ran through the turnstiles screaming and laughing. At one point we both tripped and fell straight on our backs. We just kept laughing. If we hadn't been in Hollywood the passersby would have found us strange, but this is Hollywood we're talking about. We blended right in. Once we got above ground, we wandered around for a little until we found this pizza place, called Greco's. There's nothing better than eating pizza drunk with a good friend.

June 18, 2010

Ethan almost had a breakdown. I knew he was stressed out and I knew he cared for someone who meant more to him than anything, but I didn't know how serious it actually was. I knew he skipped school several days in a row because he was too depressed to go. I knew he burned his wrist in a few places, but he kept saying it wasn't serious. I guess I just wanted to believe that, because I didn't know to handle it. I didn't want to believe lightning could strike twice, so when I saw these things with Ethan started happening, I just thought I'd up the ante. I thought I'd go over his house more, watch more television, and listen to the radio.

I thought we just needed more trips to the store to get cigarettes and junk food. That's all I wanted way back when, all I needed. I only resorted to what I resorted to after I'd called friends who couldn't make it. It was only when the whole world seemed too busy to bother with me that I started causing trouble for myself. It's crazy because when I asked Ethan why he self-harmed, he said that exact same thing. He only did it when he felt the most alone. I should have known better. Friends don't always make a difference. I had friends. You can have friends and still feel alone. You can be in choir, or dance, or color guard, or on the soccer team and still be alone. You can go to parties and watch movies on the weekend, cuddle with your girlfriend, and still feel like you have no one.

There are just those moments no one can really explain. Those moments when the worst gets the best of us. Maybe all teenagers go through it, maybe not. Maybe it's a special kind of hell reserved for the ones like Ethan and me. The ones who listen to sad songs when we don't have anything better to do. Kids who don't really have a close relationship with our parents and enjoy morose weather. It's the ones who seem happy and wear color, who feel black and empty on the inside. I felt that way a lot. That's why I should have known better.

I felt guilty when I called Ethan's house, and his dad said he'd been admitted to the hospital. I knew something was wrong and I did nothing about it. I knew he was wasting away on the inside in his room. I knew the visits couldn't last forever. The same way I couldn't fill the void forever with drinking, parties, and hookups. The void is bottomless.

I panicked immediately when I heard the news. I was transported back to when you left us. I couldn't even focus. I couldn't do or say or think anything. Fortunately, it was all for naught. Ethan is still alive. Luckily, he was admitted on a night that nothing happened. He hadn't self-harmed. He hadn't even felt particularly sad. He was actually starting to feel like his old self again.

He was admitted because someone he trusted hysterically spread word about a chilling note he wrote online. From my understanding, the note was posted to his personal blog and there was suicidal ideation involved. The next day, this 'friend of Ethan's' shows several people the note on their phone at VVHS. The chatter surrounding the note eventually reached one the teachers. The teacher alerted the school administration, and the assistant principal called the police.

Ethan wasn't on campus when the issue was reported, so the city police handled the matter. He would have been better off with the campus police. The city police department is the very definition of imbecilic. Those morons showed up at Ethan arrested in his home, hours after he wrote the post. Rather than usher him out quietly, Ethan was escorted outside in handcuffs in the early evening for all his neighbors to see. He was held on a 5150 (a 72-hour hold) at the psych ward at the local hospital. Upon Ethan's release, Immanuel, Jack, and I went straight to his house.

"It's terrible. I don't even know whom to trust. They're all spreading lies about me and this whole suicide thing. These people were supposed to be my friends," Ethan said. He was hysterical and understandably so. Immanuel and Jack each put an arm around him.

"Don't let is get to you. There are tons of rumors about me floating around," I said. "It's just immaturity. Their lives are tedious. They crave excitement, so they focus on you because you're more interesting than they are. You have us. You can trust us.

June 23, 2010

Parker graduated yesterday. I wasn't invited. There were only four tickets. Kate, his dad, and his paternal grandparents went. I wasn't upset. Parker loves his grandparents. Besides I've already been to a graduation at VVHS, my own. I'm sure this one's not too different. What is different is how Kate ordered pictures and invitations for Parker's graduation. She didn't do this for me. Oh well, he's always been her favorite. In other news, today is Jack and Ethan's graduation too. The guys and I have been going to Ethan's house almost every day to make sure he's ready for it. Sometimes we brought hookah or pot with us. Everyone has their own way of coping. We almost always put on a movie that we never ended up watching. Things seem like they're going back to being all right.

Yesterday on our way to Ethan's, Jack almost hit a kid he heard gossiping about Ethan's hospitalization. I had to stop him, but I wanted to hit the kid just as badly. Gossip is perhaps the most irritating facet of youth culture in my opinion. I'm almost positive it's worse here than anywhere else. Anyway, in addition to graduating, Ethan got news that he's been accepted into a traveling drum core for the summer. We were all happy for him and for the first time in a long time, he seems genuinely happy for himself. Also, Kate has announced she and Boethius are going on Warped Tour as soon as school ends. Surprisingly, she's asked me to come with them. I took a month off from work at Pulse to accommodate it. I don't know how I feel about being in such close quarters on the road with Kate for 30 days, but I've always loved the idea of traveling. Brian and Max's parents are letting them go alone. I don't know. I guess we'll see how everything plays out.

June 27, 2010

Kate and I had a huge fight last night. It was over the smallest thing. I had come home from a very long day at work, and she insisted I take out the trash. I did not refuse. I simply requested to take it out later. She did not abide. She demanded I do it now. I began to explain what it was like to have to walk home from work and still have to contend with homework and chores. I told her I'd do it a little later. I just wanted to rest, but my mother never lets anything, or anyone rest. She started ranting, so I turned away from her. I took my mp3 player out of my pocket, turned on music, and placed the earbuds in my ears to drown her out. I was trying to ignore her; to be calm the way Traci is always telling me to be. My sister is far more patient than me when it comes to Kate. As I started to tune her out, she ripped the earbuds out of my ears. I quietly picked them back up and placed them back in.

"Do you understand me? Listen to me!" she screamed.
I ignored her and continued concentrating on my music, so she ripped the earphones out again. This time I had had enough. I had enough of her pressuring me to meet impossible standards. I had had enough of her always telling me I was perfect one day and not good enough the next. I had enough of the little lies, her bashing my dad and praising Parker's. I had enough of her not appreciating what it took for me to wake up every day, get on the bus and go halfway across town for school then make it to work and back without a word.

I had enough of everything. I wasn't the model son. I'd made my mistakes and put strain on her. But she had done a lot worse to me. She had confused me with her ardor of praise and abhorrence. As I mentioned I was perfect one day and a disappointment the next. It all depended on whether or not she was upset about something. I had come to detest the woman who told her friends I was a spoiled brat when she ruined my chances of going to school in London.

Who the hell doesn't know how to correctly take down the time a flight leaves? My mother that's who. I was amazed that she had the nerve to cry at the airport.

She effectively ruined my only chance to go away to college and she was the one crying. She was the one getting all the attention. It was always about her. It made me nauseous. I was sick of how she wanted me to feel sympathy for her in her times of need and turned cruel or absent on me in mine. I always believed that she secretly sabotaged the trip, so she wouldn't have to let me go. She wanted me home where she could keep torturing me.

"You didn't buy those headphones, I did with my own hard-earned money, so don't touch my fucking shit." I yelled a lot at the end. She's the kind of person who can push you to yelling.

"What did you just say?" she asked. I knew I had unleashed the beast, but I simply didn't care anymore. I had spent 19 years being careful of that temperamental self-centered bitch. I loved her, but I hated her. Perhaps that's how I'm doomed to feel about all women because of her, which is only more of a reason to hate her. I repeated myself feeling justified. "Don't touch my fucking shit."

"You are a foul-mouthed, impolite, little ingrate," she said. Though she flung the word 'ingrate' around on a regular basis, it was much more vitriolic when she said it this time. "Just a failure waiting to happen."

"You're a pathetic, controlling, cold-hearted bitch. I feel sorry for you hoping to live vicariously through your child's talent." That sent her over the edge.

"Get the fuck out of my house, you little prick! All you do is waste your days partying and sleeping around."

With that I raced to the room and began packing. Sweaters, jackets, shoes, shirts, underwear, cologne - nothing in any particular order, all of it chaos just like our argument, just like my feelings. "Miserable hack," I yelled as I slammed the suitcase shut. The same suitcase she bought for our failed trip to London.

"Get out and don't ever come back!" She had followed me and began throwing things that belonged to me. Shoes, belts, pens and pencils, anything and everything. It was pure chaos.

"I hate you," I said. I put more feeling into those words than anything else I'd ever said to her in my life. I threw my keys on the floor. "You're a monster," I added.

"And you're a faggot," she said.

I had kept everything together until that moment. This was my exile, my ex-communication. I had gone towards it willingly. Then she said that and without any permission tears ran down my face. I tried to be silent and still. I couldn't believe she'd said it, then again if there's one thing, she taught me it's that there were no rules to war. And this was war.

"Oh yeah, what makes me a faggot?" I said through gritted teeth.

"You've only had few serious girlfriends and yet you have plenty of guy friends sleeping over," she said calmly. She was quite pleased with herself in saying it. She was only half-right. I've kissed two guys (as you know), which expanded my sexuality I guess, but neither of them had ever slept over. The friends she was referring to were Leo, Ezra, and Emmett. They're all straight and they're all guys I'd never even thought about as more than platonic friends. She was reaching. She always thought she knew everything. In that moment I really did feel nothing but disdain for her.

"I can't wait until you die, so I can dance on your grave," I said. I ran out of the door then as she threw a vase behind me. She missed and hit the wall. Whether she missed the flight intentionally or not, I'll never know. She continued to throw more things at me as I walked out. Some of the objects were mine, but others were her own possessions. She wasn't discerning in the slightest about what she threw. I ran with the suitcase, down the stairs, and to the parking garage.

When she wasn't looking, I took the car keys. I drove the car out down the road. Tears streamed down my face, all around my eyes, a sign of weakness. I hated it. I almost never cry. I hated myself for letting her get the best of me and I hated her more than anything. When I got a good distance away, I called my dad. He came to pick me up. He also called my mom and told her where the car was. Surprisingly, she did not decide to call the police and report it missing. It was only gone for 30 minutes anyway. Anyway, last night changed my entire life. I moved from Villa Valle back to LA in 24 hours. He isn't an easy to deal with, but anyone's easier than Kate.

July 1, 2010

I've been living with Dad and his wife Faye for a day now. So far, it's not too bad. The only major downside is they live in Leimert Park. I guess I should say we live in Leimert Park from now on. It feels so strange. There's nothing to do here and even if there was, I'd have no one to do it with. All my friends are in Villa Valle. I don't have a car, so I can't get there whenever I want. Dad said he'd take me to work, and I could spend as much time as I wanted there. That sounds perfect, but I know it won't be. I know it won't be the same. I'm so anxious. I haven't slept much or eaten much really, but it's only been a day.

I've never had a change this big before. I've handled countless rumors, outright lies, scorned ex-lovers, falling out with friends, and an emotional fling with a guy, but I don't know if I can handle this. The worst part is Kate's words are still playing in my head. *You're a faggot.* I never understood why calling someone gay or any variation thereof was supposed to be an insult. *So what?* It was meant to imply weakness, but I'm far from weak. I'm certain of that, if nothing else. I have survived too much. I don't know how that woman can even call herself my mother. And what about what I said to her? I was vicious. *How could I let her turn me into that? How could I let myself turn into that?*

July 14, 2010

I was wrong, Dad is shaping up to be as difficult to deal with as Kate. He's annoyed that I'm not working right now. I'm not working because I'm not scheduled for any shifts at Pulse. I'm not on the schedule because I took a month off for Warped Tour and all my hours were redistributed. I opened my availability back up immediately following my spat with Kate, but it was too late. It's summer and open shifts don't last long in retail. I ran into one of Parker's friends the other day and he confirmed what I already knew that I was banned from the tour. To add insult to injury, Kate asked him to replace me as roadie. I assumed I'd be disinvited after our falling out, but Kate could have at least had the decency to tell me herself, instead of allowing me to find out secondhand. Parker could have called me too. Now I'm out of work and Dad will not get off my case about it.

Faye isn't helping either. She loves spewing little insults, giving little jabs. She chimes in whenever Dad has something today and I feel like I'm getting twice the lecture. I feel like I hadn't ever accomplished anything my entire life. All because of one mistake. And who the hell was Faye to join in? I know she doesn't like me very much, but she could learn to mind her own damn business instead of making things worse. I just went through quite an ordeal, and no one seems to care. Dad keeps commenting on how I don't seem to be eating or sleeping well and yet he doesn't let up about Pulse. More stress.

For people I've spent very limited time with, Dad and Faye are sure acting like they know me. I don't know, maybe they heard stories from Traci. I know she must've relayed all the drama Kate would spill to her over the phone. All half-truths, skewed accounts. Traci probably meant well in resharing, but it's still annoying. Dad kept saying how I shouldn't have been so irresponsible as to let Kate determine anything. He's right about that at least. I know the pitfalls of Kate's plans better than anyone else. Things rarely go well for anyone involved except her.

I'm starting to feel like an idiot. On top of that the days are extremely lonely. I work sometimes, but not a lot. I try to go out to Villa Valle as much as possible, but it seems to be irritating Dad. He keeps mentioning that I need to find something productive to do with my time. Maybe he's right. He gave me a curfew of 2:00 am. I've never had a curfew in my life, but that's not what bothers me the most. The problem is it takes two hours to get to Villa Valle and back. The bus runs slower after 10:00 pm and no busses run past midnight. So, if I arrived there at six, I'd have to leave at eight just to be safe and make my shiny new curfew. I hate this so very much. I've been listening to songs by The Smiths all day. All I want to do is drown myself in sleep and Morrissey's voice.

July 23, 2010

I've been under a lot of stress. Faye still isn't helping. She's petty and labels all the food in the refrigerator. I ate one muffin that belonged to her a couple of days ago and now she labels all the food. I spoke to Traci about it, and she keeps telling me I have to deal, which isn't helping either. I just want someone to listen. She makes me feel as though what happened with our mother is entirely my fault. She'll say things like "this is the predicament you're in now." *Whatever.* I spoke to Dad, and he just told me to ignore Faye. I heard them arguing about it a bit. More fuel for her 'I hate Colin' campaign, I'm certain. Whatever. I've overheard her talking about me to her friends and family on the phone, but that's the least of my concerns.

I've been trying to balance work, friends, and my own happiness. I didn't enroll in summer session, because I planned to go on Warped Tour with Parker's band. I really hope Boethius does well, but I'm not yet past my anger towards Kate. I'm still not working much. I hate her for that. My life feels stagnant all because of this stupid tour. All because I didn't anticipate things would take the turn they did. *How could I not?* She and my sister argued like crazy when we all lived together, then Traci moved out. She had Berkeley as an option, I didn't. Pathetic. I need to start living up to that grand potential my sister, teachers, and my parents' friends are always telling I have. Dad even started in on me about it. You always encouraged me to try harder, but it never felt like you were disappointed in me in the process.

Back to the story at hand, I found out that Kate told Brian I decided to move in with my dad because I wanted to bond with him. What a load of shit! My mother is so fucking ridiculous. I'd move my entire life in 24 hours just to bond with dear old dad. I'd leave school, friends, work - everything just because I missed my father. How could anyone believe that? How could she go around telling people that? I have no reason to make my life harder than it already is. This distance is killing me.

Dad is getting stricter about what time I get home. "Don't come back past 2:00 am," he says. I've never had a curfew in my life and I'm an adult damn it!

Aside from that it takes me two hours to get to Villa Valle and two hours to get back. I'd just have to leave around 12, but no buses or trains run to his neighborhood that late. That's assuming my friends don't want to go to Pasadena or Hollywood and do something fun there. God forbid.

Kate must be loving this. I know Dad's told Traci and I'm sure Traci's spoken to Kate. No one in this family keeps anything to themselves, except for Parker. I'm sure Kate's told her beloved friends all about how horrid I was to her, especially Ms. Foley and Ms. Alleyne. The three of them formed what I like to call the evil trifecta. Trust me, the name fits. They're the three of the phoniest, gossipy, divorcées in all of Los Angeles. There was hardly a maternal instinct amongst them. Deception, petty extortion, emotional blackmail, you name it they've done it all in the name of preserving their precious egos. It's the worst on the holidays. I'm so glad I've been excommunicated because that means I won't have to endure any holiday parties with the trifecta and company. For now, I'm going to focus on the fact that summer has just begun, that and I think I know the perfect way to pay Kate back for causing me so much agony.

July 23, 2010

Kate and Boethius left for tour on the Wednesday and yesterday I threw a party of epic proportions at her house. I was only able to do so by duping my brother, which I feel a little guilty about, but this had to go off without a hitch. My plan went into motion on Tuesday. I called Parker to ask if Kate was there, she wasn't. I asked if I could come over so we could spend some time together to celebrate his graduation. He agreed. I ordered take-out from Edo Bistro, and we ate in the living room. I got stoned for the first time in that living room. It felt strange that it didn't belong to me anymore.

We spoke for a little bit, and I announced that I should probably leave before our mother returned. I got up and told him I was just going to go to the bathroom before I left. He commenced cleaning up. While he did, I walked straight down the hall to his room, instead of turning into the bathroom in the middle of the hall. Once inside I quickly searched for his backpack and stole his house keys out of them. My brother always keeps his keys in the front pocket of his backpack. Keys in tow, I hugged him and left. I knew he wouldn't go looking for them. His dad was coming to pick him up Wednesday morning. He wouldn't even need his keys, but I did.

By Wednesday afternoon I'd temporarily moved back into Kate's apartment. I told my dad I was housesitting for Leona's family while they were visiting relatives in New York. I knew he'd never check into it. He was stern but he trusted me. That's where everyone went wrong, they underestimated me. The party started around 8:00 pm. By 9:30 there were tons of people I didn't even know. I had intended it to be small but small gatherings always get too big to handle. It was fine though because we shut off the music around 10 and everyone was too drunk/stoned to cause too much of a disturbance anyway.

Even without music, my guests were still having a blast. Jack was there and he brought Vicodin. He had scored it from his cousin. Apparently that cousin had a prescription for it following a motorcycle accident but didn't really feel he needed it. Jack had the whole bottle. He and I each took one. We washed it down with was tequila. I know you're not supposed to mix pills with alcohol, but what do I have to lose? As soon as I swallowed it, I felt a warm haze and a slightly floating feeling sweep over me. My body and my mind were at rest, numb. This lasted until about one in the morning. Everyone sent texts about what a great time they had. I'm thrilled!

July 24, 2010

I was wrong about the party. Apparently, we made quite a disturbance, because Kate called to tell me off today. Her landlord informed her that due to an immense volume of noise complaints she was going to be evicted. Of course, since she's out of town she was wondering how the hell that could happen. Then I guess it all clicked, and she called me. She had no idea I stole Parker's keys. She'd locked all the windows up tightly, locked the door. She had taken my keys from me the night I left. How did I get in? Had I made duplicates? She had a million questions.

I desperately tried to hold back my laughter as she struggled to understand how I'd done what I'd done. I pretended I didn't know what in the world she was talking about. She started threatening to call the police, so I hung up, packed up, and actually headed to Leona's. Even though we hadn't been speaking regularly (especially after what I told her when I last saw her) I knew I could always go to Leona when I needed to. She let me in. I filled her in on the drama. We both agreed Kate probably wouldn't really call the cops, but you never know. I'm far less angry now. I feel like Kate and I are even. What irritates me is that I know she doesn't see it that way, but oh well. I can't make her see her mistakes. I can't make her understand. I've settled the score and that's that. Besides yesterday was my 20th birthday. I deserved a party. Jack gave me another Vicodin today. It helps more than you know.

July 28, 2010

I awoke at Leona's to find I had a voicemail on my phone. It was from Dad. He found out about the party and was absolutely irate. I played the message over and over. "I can't believe you would do this to your mother," he shouted. "If you could do it to her, you could just as easily do it to me. I don't want a vindictive person living in my house, you have to go!" I found it amusing that he was suddenly concerned with my character. I'm sure Faye must be thrilled.

I couldn't believe Dad was defending Kate, after everything she had done. I thought he would understand, but he was another person joining the Katherine Lane Fan Club. Why is it that this woman is always the victim? Why is it that no matter what she does, there are all these people willing to run to her rescue? No one rescues me. I have to rescue myself. I have to be my own savior.

I'm not complaining it just gets tiring sometimes. I'm not saying I was completely right for doing what I did, but I don't regret it. It felt like the justice I had long ached for. I suppose I'm both the hero and the villain of this story now. When I make mistakes (when any of us do) we have to make up for them. Not Katherine *fucking* Lane though. She has ex-husbands and children lining up to come to her aid. That's right. Traci and Parker have both joined our mother's fan club as well. I don't blame Parker. He's younger. He was treated differently. He spends his weekends with his dad, so he doesn't really see her as much as I do. Besides, I tricked him. I used him to get my revenge and that was awful of me. I understand why he's upset, but Traci I don't understand. My sister experienced as much of our mother's psychosis as I did. She dealt with the mood swings and severely critical remarks Kate easily dished out during arguments.

She too had been deceived and manipulated throughout her whole childhood. I mean Kate used to always tell us how heart-broken she was when our father left her for a co-worker (not Faye, this was an earlier girlfriend). She told us that he ruined their marriage, and never tried to win her back. One day, Traci summoned the courage to ask

Dad about it. He admitted that he cheated on our mother with a co-worker. He said he'd cheated because he felt distant from her. He worked hard all day long, while she lounged at home. She had just received her bachelor's but hadn't found a job. Instead of working, she was spending the afternoons shopping with Traci, running up his credit cards.

He never said it was right or okay to cheat, but I guess he had his reasons at the time. Contrary to my what Kate said, he did try to win her back. He tried to apologize and makes things right, but she refused to speak to him. He brought flowers and cand. He was still paying all our bills, even though he was staying with a friend. It didn't make a difference. When Dad discovered Kate had begun dating Parker's father, he gave up. Kate never told us any of that. In her version of things, she was a saint, and he was the merciless adulterer who tore our family apart.

Traci knew all of this. This was just one of Kate's many fabrications. How could she still take our mother's side? She knew what I endured firsthand and somehow didn't think I had any right to get back to our mom. I was in utter disbelief. More to the point, I may have to find a new place to live now. Kate won in the end. Fitting, I suppose. I couldn't calm my nerves. I feel more alone than ever. I feel like I don't belong in this family.

I took a shower at Leona's, but I couldn't calm my nerves. I was composed on the outside, but a complete wreck on the inside. I couldn't even get the point where I'd be able to write this to you, so I took a little help. I asked Jack for more Vicodin. This time I took two. I went completely numb, but in a pleasant way. We took the bus to a vintage store I know of in East Hollywood. There was a fashion show scheduled. Local designers produced all the clothes. Bright, flashy, tantalizing costumes were everywhere. I knew this was something I wanted to be a part of. I was never any good at creating art, aside from dressing. And maybe that was an art. Perhaps I could be a human canvas.

August 1, 2010

I decided to go home today. Leona's mother extended the invitation for me to stay at their place indefinitely, but I rescinded the offer for obvious reasons. Also, before I left, Jack gave me two more Vicodin for the road. I drank it with beer at his place. Warm haze, slightly floating, I was resting again, numb again. Unfortunately, it wore off by the time I actually got home. It was hours before I had to face Dad. He was furious at first, more so that I didn't come home right away, but he listened to me. Once he'd heard me out about everything, he said he understood. He also said it wasn't right for me to do what I did, which I already knew. He gave me a speech about revenge and included that famous quote by Gandhi "an eye for an eye makes the whole world blind."

This was a little ironic to hear him say since he was once in the Navy, but I guess since he didn't serve during any war, he's allowed to be a pacifist. He said he was still pretty damn upset with me, but that he wasn't going to kick me out. I decided I had to do something to prevent Kate and Parker from getting thrown out as well. I went online and found the landlord's number. I called and made him aware of who I was. I took full responsibility for throwing the party. Kate isn't even back yet, but when she does get back, she's going to discover she's no longer getting evicted. One wrong, righted.

Traci still won't answer my calls, but whatever. This had nothing to do with her anyway. Speaking of calls, I received a not so surprising one from my maternal grandmother, Jeanne. We call her gran. In spite of the stormy and intermittent nature of her relationship with Kate, our ties have never been severed. Whenever there is serious family dysfunction, my gran intervenes. She's the only living grandparent I have left, so hearing from her is always appreciated regardless of the circumstances.

"Bonjou [2] Colin," she said warmly in her thick Lucian accent.

"Bonjou," I said demurely. As I mentioned before, I can't speak much Kwéyòl. I can, however, understand bits and pieces from Kate speaking it around me in childhood. She ensured I took French in high school. Though Kwéyòl is not exactly intelligible with standard French, knowing it helps to break down meanings.

"Bon fèt monchè [3]," my gran said. She was the only person in my family who wasn't too angry with me to wish me happy birthday. I thanked her for the well wishes. I knew that even though she had remembered my birthday and sounded sweet upon introduction, that this could just as easily turn if I didn't play my cards right. After exchanging basic pleasantries, she dove right in.

"I've spoken to your manman, [4]" she said. "She's missed you. She's just a little upset because of the party you threw." I was sure Kate gave her the watered-down version of the story. I'm sure she did not include the screaming and the throwing of random objects, but I'm also sure my grandmother knew this. Also, she usually did not try to play mediator, so I decided to hear her out.

"I know. I felt like she pushed me though. There's an entire side to the story that I'm certain she did not make you aware of," I replied.

"I'm sure of that Colin, but you must still make peace with her. She is still your mother and though she can be difficult you will only have one," she said.

"I know, but she is so unreasonable!"
"I agree. She has to be more understanding. She was far from obedient when she was young. You only have one manman, you mustn't forget to honor her though," she said.

---

[2] Good morning; Hello (Kwéyòl; from the French 'bonjour').

[3] Happy birthday (Kwéyòl; from the Fr. bon for 'good' and fête meaning 'party');
  My dear (Kwéyòl; Fr. mon cher).

[4] Mother (Kwéyòl; Fr. maman).

She was right on both accounts sometimes older generations forget what it was like to be young. I don't know if I believe in generational curses, but maybe some of us are really we're doomed to repeat our parents' mistakes. Kate rebelled against her family, now I'm rebelling against her.

August 6, 2010

I started the day off taking three Vicodin. I tried talking to Lexie, but she was busy. So was everyone else. I can't rely on anyone to fix my problems anyway. I don't know how to fix them on my own yet, so I took three Vicodin and drank it with water this time. I figured continuing to take it with alcohol would be a little too much. I started with one but took two more because I didn't feel anything. Once I upped the dose, I was loose. I began playing the new Arcade Fire album, *The Suburbs*.

I don't think you ever heard of them. They're amazing. I love every single song. Loose and ready for the Bloomfest LA concert. There were several different bands playing. We only went to see Group Love and Voxhaul Broadcast. We arrived early, like around 4:00 pm. Those bands weren't scheduled to play until way later, so of course Troy and I decided to hunt for a place to buy beer. I persuaded a tourist to buy it for us, feigning that I had left my ID at home. It would have been far more exciting if we didn't have to walk seven blocks just to find a place. Little Tokyo is full of great bars and restaurants, but almost completely devoid of liquor stores. We ended up going to a market.

The cashier kind of looked at us oddly but once my license scanned, she didn't say anything. After purchasing it came the task of trying to figure out where we were going to drink. This is biggest downside to not being 21 is not having always having a designated place to imbibe. I had to get inventive. We stopped by a local mall. The letters were mostly in Japanese. It wasn't very big but there were a large number of people in it. It was a small outdoor mall. There were about 7 or 8 stores, spread evenly on two floors, and there was a large open courtyard in the center. We searched the ground floor for a restroom – no luck. We searched the second floor for a restroom – no luck still. Then we walked into a store and asked a clerk where we could find one. The clerk gave us directions and when we walked back up to the second floor, we still couldn't find it.

We went about the mall hurriedly in circles before finally locating the restrooms via little sign that stuck out from the far-left side corner of the complex. We raced to it only to discover it was locked. Just as we were giving up someone walked out. Troy grabbed the door handle, and we walked in. However, to our horror this was one of those split restrooms with men and women's sides and both doors were locked. We knocked but no one seemed to be inside. Troy, who had been relatively relaxed for Troy, started to say that perhaps it was a good idea we left. I felt we had come too far to give in.

I ignored him and pulled out a gift card from my wallet. The card had already been used and so it wouldn't matter if it were damaged in our scheme. I slid the card in between the lock and the door jam, pulled down and voila! The door was opened. Troy was amazed and I was confused because I thought everyone knew how to do that. I mean it's an elementary trick. I first saw Kate do it one time when Parker accidentally locked himself out of his room. Once inside we headed to a stall and cracked open out 24-ounce cans. We purchased two each. We sipped the first laughing about how crazy it was that we were in a public restroom drinking.

"I still can't believe you opened the door with a rewards card," Troy said.

"Haven't you learned by now not to underestimate me my dear Mr. Sanz?" Troy was one of the few friends who never minded it when I gloated. Probably cause he's known me for so long. I'm not as arrogant a person as I seem sometimes. I guess that's the kind of thing you only get to know if you've known me since I was 14, the way Troy has.

As Troy finished his can of beer and I was halfway done with mine, the door burst open. I ran to a corner to hide my legs from view, but it was too late. A man and his friend were chuckling. It must have seemed as though Troy and I went into the stall for some afternoon fun. They didn't say anything but "oh there are two people in there" and Troy just started laughing. His laughter triggered my own and suddenly we were cackling uncontrollably. I walked back towards Troy so that my legs were in sight again from under the stall. I downed the rest of my can and started the second. We heard the men exit the restroom. Relief washed over us.

Troy was still laughing when they did. It took him a while to stop. He started on his second and by the time we had both finished it was almost time for Group Love's set. We strolled out of the restroom, out of the mall and back down the street. We spent the rest of the night dancing and smoking out there in the open with Immanuel and Immanuel's friend. It was her cannabis. It was magnificent. The night was magnificent.

August 13, 2010

Immanuel's friend threw a party tonight and I went. I took four Vicodin and drank whiskey all night. I probably shouldn't have, but that numbness ...I needed it. I ran into Gisele, and I didn't expect to. We spoke. It was messy at first. She took me outside without a warning and we didn't stop talking for about 45 minutes straight. We exchanged all our worries and concerns. As I started to come clean about the other girls, she stopped me, said she didn't want to know. I let her know I understood why in that quiet understanding kind of way. We laughed at ourselves, at how silly we had been to be afraid. We went for a walk. As we ventured in the darkness beneath trees together, something came over us both.

     We started out just holding hands. We both had a lot to drink by then. I had started to feel warm and tingly inside. I wondered if she felt the same way. We stopped in front of a house somewhere down the street from the party. We were facing each other, our hands still linked. Her skin was soft and smooth like shea butter. Her hands broke with mine and found their way around my waist. I slipped my hands around hers bringing her in closer. Next thing I know, we were kissing. She felt so warm, and we were so drunk that I could taste the alcohol. She slid her hands under my shirt and caressed my abs. I'm quite proud of my physique, if nothing else, and seeing that she was enjoying it made me even prouder. The whole time we were silently exploring each other. I started mimicking her movements, caressing her.

     To everyone else we probably looked like too drunken idiots groping at each other in the middle of the night. To me, it was uniquely intimate and lustful at the same time. I found myself craving the connection I had been deprived of, with someone I wasn't even sure I wanted. Maybe we were just pushing our limits. Maybe this was just about sex. We didn't end up going all the way, but it was all I could do not to think about was undressing her. Her mom called to summon her home. Even though she 18, she was still in high school, and it was getting late. I had started to regret the other girls

I was seeing before left, then I remembered why I turned to them in the first place.

I was terribly afraid of being truly vulnerable with someone again and sublimating my fear by hooking up. I was selfish for letting things get this far tonight. When she said she had to go we went back to the party. She left and I stayed until I passed out. When I woke up it was 7:00 am. I went home and that's where I am now. In my room (my dad's old office), on my bed (a pull-out sofa), writing this to you. Not certain what it says about me or who I am. Not certain if I should even give a damn.

August 17, 2010

There's good news and bad news. The good news is I've been working more regularly. Dad isn't so upset with me anymore, so I've been going to Villa Valle a lot. It kind of feels like I never left. The bad news is I thought I had my fill of awkward run-ins, and I was wrong. Apparently, the universe has nothing better to do then fuck with me. What makes me say this you ask? I ran into Duncan yesterday. I was minding my own business, and he literally appeared out of nowhere. I had just finished shopping at some cool thrift stores in Silver Lake. I was walking down Rowena Avenue, and he drove up next to me. He was in a car with Emmett, some other friend of theirs, and a very pretty girl.

"Where are you going?" he yelled ecstatically.

I was less than thrilled to see him, but also surprised. I didn't have a lot to time to react or make up a lie either, so I told him the truth. "I'm just headed home," I said.

"Get in," he said motioning me over.

I shook my head. "I'm alright. I could use the walk."

"Come on Colin, please." He said. He puckered his bottom lip. He sounded so sincere. I really didn't feel like it, and I probably shouldn't have, but I did. Somehow, I also let him talk me into eating with them. I made him aware that I had no money, but he said that wouldn't be a problem, he'd pay. I politely refused. He insisted. He's not the kind of guy to take no for an answer usually, but something about this seemed urgent. It seemed like he wasn't just trying to get me to have lunch. We went to the Morrison on Los Feliz. After we ordered drinks and placed our food orders with the server, I learned what his big news was.

"You know, I'm leaving for the Marines, right?" Duncan said. Emmett was checking out one of the female bartenders and their friend was making out with the pretty girl who I guess is his girlfriend, so it felt like just Duncan and I at the table. I couldn't believe Duncan, whom I hadn't seen or heard from in months, was sitting here telling me he was going to leave Villa Valle. He wasn't going to be a drive, a bus, or cab ride away anymore. He was going off somewhere to become an entirely different person. This is the same guy who called me incandescent. That same guy was sitting here telling me he was going to go away, and I hated him for it. I felt like I was losing something, and I didn't know what or why. I felt like I had just been punched straight in the gut. I felt like I should be bleeding or losing my balance or something. I felt all of these things sitting down calmly next to him in a chair. The food arrived and I downed my drink. I needed it. He ordered me another. I took a sip and just said what I was thinking.

"I can't believe you're leaving," I said.

"I know," he replied.

"We're probably never going to see each other again."

"I mean, I wouldn't say never."

"Let's be realistic here."

"I am being realistic. I can't say that I'm never coming back."

"Okay not for a long time then, might as well be never."

"I know." All I could think about was how much this sucked. I wished he'd said something other than 'I know.' I wanted him to tell me where the hell he'd been and why he'd stopped talking to me. I wanted to know whether he was really working as a secret go-go boy in WeHo. I wanted to know why he thought he had the right to spring all of this on my randomly. I wasn't going to say any of that though. Why would I? He was leaving for the Marines soon anyway.

"Let's just eat and pretend everything is alright," I said.

"Isn't that called living in denial?" he said.

"Not really, it'll be true eventually. Let's call it speeding up the process."

"Very well then." We ate in virtual silence for a bit, then Emmett mulling over his coconut curry told a joke that made us all laugh. We all made small talk afterward, until everyone finished eating. There were smiles all around at our table, in the dim lighting at the Morrison. Every single one was authentic except mine and maybe

Duncan's. I couldn't tell.

I didn't want to be able to. The rich, warm tones of the restaurant seeped into us as our food settled. Emmett and Duncan and their friend split the bill and then we left. He dropped everyone else off before me, so it was just us at the end of the night. We made more small talk at first and then things grew serious.

We talked about how his mother was going to miss him. She wasn't the only one. I was going to miss him terribly. I still didn't know why, so I didn't say anything. We kept chatting until we reached the street where my dad lives. I couldn't believe Duncan actually drove me all the way to Leimert Park. I had him stop a few houses down, so my dad and Faye wouldn't be alerted to my arrival. I unbuckled my seatbelt and stared at him for a moment. He stared right back at me and neither of us moved.

"I guess this is where we part ways," he said.

"Yeah," I said. There was a long paused and then suddenly something came over me. It was a deep challenging impulse, and you know how I feel about challenges. I couldn't hold back. There was no reason to anymore. So, I just said it. "Hey since you're leaving, I guess there's no reason not to tell you, you're an asshole."

"What, why?" he said. He sounded genuinely surprised.

"Because you stopped talking to me after the DTF text and now this. You decide to spring this news on me casually."

"I'm sorry. I didn't think you'd care. Why are you so upset? I heard you had quite a good amount of adventure after we lost contact?"

"Lost contact?"

"Ok after I bailed out of talking to you"

"Better," I said a little calmer. "What did you hear?"

"Stuff." I hate it when people are vague. He was doing it intentionally. We went back and forth like that for a while. With me asking for specifics and him obfuscating his answers. "It wasn't anything memorable," he said. He looked down at his feet and then around the car a bit. The frost from the night air chilled the outside of our window. Little beads of condensation formed and streamed down like raindrops.

"I'm serious I didn't pay attention to it. Haven't you figured this out yet? Dude, I'm in love with you. I love you, regardless of who you stick in."

I was stunned. I didn't know what to make of it. Were these parting words a genuine confession or just sweet nothings? I couldn't help but be annoyed by it. My chest swelled and I released a breath. I wanted out of the car so badly. I wanted to run down the street screaming. None of this made sense. He was a sporadic, albeit fun presence in my life, but love? I was forced to face the fact that no one had said anything to me of that magnitude since Amelia. Leona cared, but it wasn't enough. Alessandra, Chloe, and Kasey – they all wanted me some version of me but not the real me, in my entirety. The same could be said for the bookstore clerk, the Canadian exchange student, and the artsy goth girl I had hooked up with. None of these dalliances ever came close to turning into love. I couldn't even fathom how Duncan had concluded that he loved me. Maybe he meant as a friend? The mixture of confusion and deep-seated curiosity, compelled me to speak up.

"I care about you," I said. "I just have a lot going on and didn't know how to express that in a meaningful way until now." I couldn't quite say I was in love, but I knew I liked him as more than a friend and I did care about him. That's why I didn't mind all the inappropriate texts. It was all starting to make sense to me. "I would've said something sooner, but I assumed you only wanted attention. It wasn't you. It was me."

"Classic," he said. His voice was shaky and filled with emotion. I could tell he was trying his hardest to stifle any outbursts. I hadn't realized how invested he was in whatever this was shaping up to be. It wasn't my intention to rely on such a tired cliché to explain myself, but it was the truth.

"I know how it sounds, but I'm serious," I said.

"I know," he said. Those words hung in the air for a while. We just sat there in silence processing the exchange. Then he spoke again. "You should probably..."

"Get going, yeah," I said, finishing his sentence before he could. I turned to unlock the door, but he got to it before me, then another sudden rush hit me. I turned back and gave him a passionate kiss on the lips. In that moment, we were unbound by any restrictions, worries, insecurities or past issues. It was pure, light, human contact. We kissed in his car, two houses down from my dad's driveway for what felt like forever. We could have easily been caught by my dad, Faye, or one of their neighbors, but I didn't care about any of that. I ran my fingers through his hair and held the back of his head as I kissed him. He placed on the small of my back and pressed into me as our lips met. The birds slept in their little nests and the trees swayed from the cool August breeze. I heard "A Perfect Sonnet" by Bright Eyes streaming through the radio, even though the radio was off. Then like all good things, it came to an end. Lips parted and we settled back into our seats. I figured that was as good a time as any to make my exit.

"Goodbye," I said soft and low.

"Bye," he said. I walked down to the house and up the driveway. I tried not to think about what any of it meant or what I had to do next. I waltzed over to my pull-out sofa and fell asleep.

August 24, 2010

Painkillers are amazing. I can't believe I never tried them prior to recent events. I've been depressed since I moved out of Kate's (maybe even before that if I'm being honest). Duncan's going away is really hitting me too. I took four vikes today and drank it with cheap whiskey I copped at a sketchy local liquor store. Liquor stores around here will sell alcohol to you with no ID, as long as you're bold enough. Dad and Faye were at work most of the day. Dad at the restaurant, and Faye at her job at the accounting firm. I don't believe she's an accountant, but I'm not really sure what she does, so let's just say she's an accountant. I was blitzed the whole afternoon. I had no reason not to be.

Things aren't getting any better. I'm charming and witty and fun and magnetic and then I'm not. I'm not because I screw it up, or someone else screws it up. I don't know. I'm certain of the things I don't want, I'm just not certain of what it is I do want. I guess that makes it difficult for people who try to be a part of my life, and I'm mean a serious part, not just someone to drink or smoke with. Maybe that made it difficult for Gisele. She's been texting but I haven't replied. I hate how I'm this paradox. Resented and beguiled and yet adored. Discarded and disregarded and yet still implored. It's not cut and dry either, the people that claim to love, want, need me the most almost always end up hating me.

The reasons they do are almost always the same facets they found fascinating in the first place. Kasey liked that I was a free spirit. I am wonderfully awful. I am an unhealthy desire. Leona called me that once. I'm so tired of thinking about her and everyone and everything. This year wasn't supposed to turn out like this. I wasn't supposed to get tangled into shit. I wasn't supposed to care about him. Not too long before that I loved Leona. How the hell did I get here? It's not even that he's guy. It's just that I didn't know I felt that deeply until I was saying it.

I've been so out of touch with myself. Now there's nothing I can do. I took the vikes, drank some, and then slept for four hours. When I awoke, I felt like shit, but I went out anyway. As soon as I got to Villa Valle, I called Immanuel. We walked through the park and smoked cigarettes. I took a deep, long breath. I inhaled all the sweet toxins and exhaled. I went by Kate's hoping to speak with her. She wasn't home. On my way around the block, I ran into an unfamiliar face. She was a relatively pretty woman, about 5'6," with reddish brown hair and light brown eyes. Her name was Eva. She told me she recognized me. I was certain we'd never met, but she insisted.

"I know your mom, Kate," she said.

"Oh yeah," I said.

Even when we weren't speaking, Kate would do anything to boast. It was kind of nice to know she was still talking about me. It was also strange though, because I half-expected her to act like I'd died. I continued talking to Eva. She invited me to wait it out at her place, until Kate got home. I wasn't going to at first, but I was still a little buzzed from the vikes and the alcohol. I didn't want to be caught out on the street like that.

She walked me down the street to her apartment. She lived in an older building, with only four units, including hers. Her apartment was kitschy, but nicely decorated. The walls were pastel pink, and the floors were made of rich oak wood. She poured herself a glass of white zinfandel and offered me one. We drank and talked a little more. She quickly began hitting on me. She called me handsome and commented on how delicious I smelled – all in the span of what seemed like 15 seconds. I could tell where this was leading. I was aware enough to know and high enough not to care. *Why should I care?*

I had experienced radical change in the past few months. I told a guy I had feelings for him. I opened myself up completely and it was all for nothing. I knew it wasn't going to amount to anything before I kissed him, and I did it anyway. Traci was the smart one, Parker was the prodigy, and I was the screw up. I was a magnet for drama and chaos. *So what?* As she moved in closer, I noticed a photo on the shelf behind her. In it, she was posed with an older gentleman on what looked like the Santa

Monica Pier.

"Who's that?" I asked motioning over to the picture.

"That's Salvatore," she said, as if I knew who she was talking about.

"How do you know Salvatore?" I said. Immediately after I asked, I wished I hadn't. It was too late. In my naïveté I assumed him to be a blood relative at first. *Perhaps he was her older brother, or a cousin. Maybe her uncle?* He wasn't.

"Sal's my deadbeat husband," she said flatly. I should have backed out and left her apartment straight away, but I didn't. Instead, I looked around and could see no clear sign that her husband lived there. There weren't any men's shoes on her shoe rack. When I went to her bathroom, I failed to find any cologne, or aftershave lingering around. There weren't even any articles of men's clothing in her closet. I figured they were probably separated, but I didn't pry. I can't recall if she was wearing a wedding ring. It didn't matter.

Nothing was stopping me. I felt reckless and hollow, and I wanted to feel something else, anything else. If I'm being perfectly honestly, I wanted to be wanted by someone. So, I took off my jacket and lowered the straps on her dress from her shoulders. I caressed her cheek and kissed her neck. She kissed my jaw line, wrapped her hands around my head. Her dress slid down her taut torso and around her waist. She unbuttoned my gray button-down shirt. We French-kissed, hot and steady, and then I took off her bra. She clawed the small of my back. I slipped off her panties. She bit just below my collarbone, and my knees almost gave way. She unbuckled my belt came, and eventually we were lying on her living room floor enraptured in heat and lust. She's married, but that's not my business. This was a one-time thing. Another all too fitting Oscar Wilde quote popped into my head as I left her place, *my existence is a scandal.*

September 7, 2010

Today was my first day back at school. The first day back at Villa Community College after summer vacation is just about the largest social gathering attended by 18–25-year-olds in the city. It's also utterly predictable. Scores of little groups meet to brag about what they did, gossip what someone else did, and bitch about their classes. Every day after that is like one big fashion show with a million smoke breaks in between. It's ridiculous. The stories are all the same. Everyone goes to Palm Springs, if not they went to Mexico, if not they went to Vegas. Everyone goes to Vegas again for their 21st birthdays. Villa Valle where the middle class goes broke trying to live like the upper class. Not me.

Don't get me wrong, I've definitely participated in the spectacle, but this time, not me. Not after the past year. Not after everything that's happened. I've decided I don't want to be a part of it anymore. I'm just going to sit back and watch it all. I've spent the few years of my life building connections, becoming more and more *socially relevant* as Troy calls it. All for what? It all means nothing. Ridiculous. It's nice to be known, but it's better to be loved. I haven't felt loved in so long. Maybe I'm not meant for that. Maybe I'm just meant to be idealized and desired until either I get bored, or they get bored. It never goes anywhere anyway. Nowhere real at least. - I did a lot of insane things this summer – all fodder for the rumor mill. I've already heard exaggerated versions of my antics. Maybe I should have gone to Palm Springs.

I spent the day laughing and smoking. Laughing whenever I heard a 'didn't you' story followed by some horrendously overblown thing I certainly did not do and smoked in between classes. 'You threw a party at your mom's with like 100 people there and there was a huge fire, right?' Sure, and everybody miraculously survived. 'You broke up with that Gisele girl from Truman, because she was pregnant and wasn't sure who the father was, right?' Yup, we even went on a talk show.

Roll my eyes and smoke another cigarette. Being socially relevant can be a fucking drag. I've switched to smoking Turkish Royals and they're quite tasty. If my lungs are going to die because it's the only way I can cope with moronic questions about my life, I at least need it to be an enjoyable process. Luckily this only happened between classes. My classes were the only plus side.

I have great classes. I'm taking Psychology 105: Human Sexuality, English 103: Creative Writing, and French 101. I probably shouldn't be taking the latter course since I know a good deal of French already, but I want an easy A. Besides at this point I've completed all my major requirements and general ed courses, all I have left to cover is math. I hate math. My major is Political Science by the way. It's called a low it's a unit major at Villa Community, because there aren't too many classes to take for it. Anyway, French is my favorite class so far and not just because it's easy. I've already met some really cool people in it. There's Beau, Lola, and Portia.

Beau is a photographer, but not the condescending douchey kind. Lola and Portia take all their classes together and got to the gym together. They're insightful and funny and go back and forth with Beau and me. I'm glad I met new people. Lexie and I usually help each other get through the minutia of going to Villa Community, but she isn't enrolled this semester. We talked some about what she's been going through last night. She made me feel like I helped. I wish I could help myself that same way I help her. Anyway, every Monday I have Psych 105. I suspect it'll be my second favorite course. Tomorrow, I have English 103. I've always loved writing, who knows how it'll be.

September 23, 2010

I was right, French is hands down my favorite class. Psych 105 is a close second. The latter has helped me fully come to terms with sexual identity in the wake of these lingering feelings for Duncan. Sexuality is a huge and complicated spectrum. Bi-curious, bisexual, fluid – call me whatever you want, just don't call me the wrong thing. I'm not confused. I love being with girls, but I would definitely consider being with a guy. Consider being the operative word. It's no big deal. It's not much of a surprise either. I've always been attracted to different body types – tall girls, short girls, thin, curvaceous, I've run the gamut. Now I know that my capacity for attraction extends beyond gender.

Accepting this feels great, but it doesn't solve that nagging little question of why I can't seem to make it work with anyone. I'm sure I'm going about things the wrong way though. That's a step in the right direction at least. Self-awareness if grand, but I'm not quite ready to change any of my behaviors yet. Fortunately, I'm not alone, I have Beau from my French class. He's pretty awesome. We smoke cigarettes together during our 30 min breaks from class. All twice a weeknight classes get a 30-minute break. We usually just talk shit. We've shared a few glory stories and some horror stories too. He never asks me about any rumors. He's had to have heard them, but he doesn't seem to care.

I suppose there isn't much need for him to speculate. I'm usually forthcoming about what I did since the last time we talked and whom I may have slept with. He's just as honest with me. He's a real person. It's so refreshing to know real people. Lola is real as well. She says exactly what she thinks. She isn't rude about it, she's just direct. Portia's real when she's paying attention. I haven't really spoken to anyone besides them, Lily, Leo, and Ezra. Jack and the guys have to finish high school. I can't sit around taking Vicodin all day and drowning my sorrows in booze.

I have to suck it up and save the energy for parties on the weekends like everyone else my age. This is called growing up. Wake up, deal with bullshit, go to school, go to work, sleep, repeat. Last Thursday Beau and I skipped class and sparked up a jay at the park across the street. We decided to make that our Thursday ritual. He said that officially makes us burnouts. I agreed and told him about Eva. He congratulated me.

"Sounds like a moral grey area. For all you know they could be separated. Right or wrong, take is as a feat," he said.

Maybe youth is about screwing up, doing all you can to live life to its fucking fullest before you have to go. I told Beau about my English 103 instructor, Professor Eriksson. He's Swedish but speaks English brilliantly. I've missed more than a couple of assignments and he's allowed me to make them up – even though there is generally no allowance for make- up assignments. Beau says he's seen Professor Eriksson around and thinks he might be gay.

"You should try flirting with him," Beau said teasingly, "then find what you can get away with." *Perhaps I should flirt with Professor Eriksson. He's cute and it would be a relatively harmless experiment.*

October 12, 2010

Last week in English 103 we learned our professor is gay. No big shock there, Beau called it. Anyway, once I found this out Beau and I started joking about how I could use it to my advantage. Then I really thought about it and decided to try it out. I missed a test. I missed a test because I decided to skip and drink wine and smoke cigarettes with Immanuel and a couple girls he knew instead. As I mentioned before Professor Eriksson expressed to everyone that there would be no-make ups from the very first day of class. I've always liked a challenge. I decided to visit him during his office hours today, see if I could actually flirt to get my way, like Beau and I had discussed.

I know flirting can be a rather abstract concept, so I'll try my best to paint you a picture of how things went. He was alone in his office. I knocked on the door and he urged me to come in. I walked in. He took a seat and offered me one. Before sat down, before I even attempted ask him if I could make up the test, I complimented his sweater. It was a blue and black argyle pullover. I didn't just say "hey nice sweater." I said, "I really like this sweater of yours," in an unmistakably warm tone. I also made sure to make eye contact while saying it. He smiled sheepishly and thanked me. I casually unbuttoned the top two buttons of my shirt. I could just hear Beau screaming *show some skin*, in my head as I did it.

I raised my hand up around my neck and down the top part of my back, then sighed and dropped it back down again. This was all meant to sync up with my excuse, overworked college student who just needs a break on this one little exam. "Sorry," I said, "I'm just so tired from work." I took a seat. "Anyway, I wanted to talk to you about the exam I missed. I meant to come to class, but my job scheduled me for a shift. I couldn't get out of it, and I would have arrived after you would have started instruction. I didn't want to interrupt. My manager knows I have you on Tuesdays and Thursdays, so it must some sort of silly mistake on their part."

"I don't know, I don't condone students missing exam dates for any reason,"

Professor Eriksson said sternly. He wasn't going to be persuaded so easily. Was he challenging me or setting boundaries? I couldn't quite tell.

"I know and I wouldn't have under any other circumstances, but it really couldn't be helped. Seriously where'd you get that sweater?" I was trying to break through his tough exterior, but he was unfazed.

"Mr. Prescott we're supposed to be here discussing your missed exam, not my wardrobe or where I go shopping," he said. I wasn't going to give up the that easily either. I needed to take this exam.

"I know, I'm sorry," I said. I was faking earnestness as best as I could. Then I switched to a more casual tone. "I've just got a thing for well-tailored clothes, especially sweaters. I shouldn't even worry about it though. It wouldn't look as good on me." If outright flirting didn't work, flattery might.

"What makes you say that?" He said. He was giving way a bit. It was the opening I had been hoping for. I ceased the opportunity.

"Well, your build for one. I mean I don't know what you do to keep fit, but whatever it is it works, that and the color scheme." Professor Eriksson laughed a bit and looked away then asked what I meant about the color scheme.

"The navy blue in the sweater just compliments your eyes so well. It wouldn't have the same effect with mine."

"Well thanks," he said still not able to look at me directly. He was blushing. It was working. "But back to the point Mr. Prescott." He was maintaining the air of formality required for a teacher-student dynamic. But I estimated that he wasn't that much older than me. There's no way he wasn't at least mildly curious about whether I was attracted to him or not.

"Ok, but before we continue, can you just call me Colin?" I slid off the jacket I was wearing and hung it across the back of my chair.

"Sure, I suppose that couldn't hurt," he said. "Colin, I really like you."

"I really like you too Professor Eriksson," I said as I flashed my signature smile. I was straddling the fence between innocent student and devilish seductor. I knew it was inappropriate, but I loved every second of it. It's not like anything was going to happen.

"Yes, well I'm glad, because I enjoy having you in class. You participate well and the work you've completed so far is great, but that's when you choose to come to class. You need to improve your attendance and complete everything if you intend to pass this course."

"I know Professor Eriksson. I'm definitely going to improve."

"No more excuses?" He asked leaning over the desk. This was a gesture clearly meant to display seriousness. He was attempting to be intimidating, but it hadn't worked on me.

"Scouts honor," I said smiling again and leaning in just as close. He didn't expect that and leaned back quickly.

"You can make up the exam then." I thanked him and extended my hand to shake his. When we went for it, I held his hand a little longer than usual but not too long. Then I smiled, grabbed my jacket and let go again. It was subtle and it worked. I could sense how tense he felt. It was a good kind of tension. I've always had a bad habit of toying with authority figures. This is probably because Kate was never consistently authoritative. I was usually able to talk my way out of punishments when I was younger, or at least get the severity lessened.

When I got older, I just started disobeying her. Now my morals are all skewed and I'm repeating that pattern with other authority figures. I took that from my Psych 105 class. Now that I'm fully aware of my powers of persuasion with both sexes and more comfortable with it, I'm using it to the fullest extent. If I'm such magnetic, incandescent, charming person I might as well use it to my advantage. Use it, 'til it's all gone. In fact, I've already started doing so. I also missed an important paper in Psych 105 and got my due date postponed for a week by flirting with the teacher's assistant. The only thing is now that paper has to be amazing. Whatever. This just reminds me of high school. I can put in minimal effort and probably still get an A. It's odd, so much has changed, and yet so much has stayed the same.

October 14, 2010

I arrived at school at around 6:15 pm though French doesn't start until 7:00. I showed up early so Beau and I could complete our ritual – smoking hash in the men's room – lovely burnouts. I don't know, I'd like for things to be different, but I'm not sure if that's possible. I get the feeling that no matter what all the shit I've had to endure is just going to repeat. With or without my permission there'll be chaos. If some external force doesn't create it, I'll create it myself. That's what I do when I get bored or lonely or feel trapped, I create chaos. It's beautiful in a poetic sense, yet awful to live through. Sometimes I feel like I'm like a character in a soap opera whose been given all the most interesting storylines. My life is all disaster and tragedy, with intermittent intervals of joy.

It's all so trite and tiresome. I made up with Kasey yesterday and even that didn't feel as good as it should have. Though perhaps that was because I didn't really feel like he forgave me wholeheartedly. Not that I deserved it, I just wanted it. We really can't always get what we want. It's the cruelest law of nature. He did say he never stopped believing I was a good person. I was nice to hear that, even if I'm not sure that he meant it. Hell, I'm not even sure what I believe concerning the matter. All I know is I how I feel in this very moment, and I feel I'm just going through the motions. I appreciate what I have, but it doesn't stop me from missing what I don't. Talking to Kasey again made me face another of my demons, my unresolved feelings for Duncan. I put what happened with us last on the backburner. I tried to bury it underneath Vicodin and drinking and sleeping with Kate's neighbor. There was no escaping it. I flushed the rest of this vikes I had today.

October 28, 2010

In keeping with the theme of last week, triteness and peacemaking, Kate and I spoke today. She said Eva told her I came by looking for her. I laughed. Eva must be wondering why she hadn't heard from me. Whatever. It's not like she's going to tell Kate about u and ask for my number. And back to Kate, honestly, our conversation didn't go exactly as I expected, but it wasn't too far from how I assumed things would go either. In her eyes I had behaved like Judas Iscariot, Cain to my brother's Abel, and the prodigal son all in one – shades of her Catholic upbringing. In her eyes, she had given me everything. She had given me the best she could give, and I rejected it. Not only that, but I also rejected her, denounced her as my mother time and again, until it was too much to bear. She was sorry for what she said and how she acted the night I moved out, but it did not warrant my throwing a party at her apartment that almost got her evicted. Those were the expressions and characterizations I saw coming. What I did not see coming was her explaining herself.

"It wasn't easy being twice divorced and having to raise three kids. I feel anxious all the time. I'm stressed about the bills that alimony doesn't help me pay and covering all of your and Parker's needs. I'm under pressured to succeed in my field, especially being a woman of color. It's a lot," she said.

She went onto to say how much she missed me. I had never thought Kate would miss me if I left home. I hated to admit it, but part of me missed her as well. She is my mother after all. She's the only one I'll ever have, as my grandmother had put it. It was dicey, but it wasn't excruciating. I still got high with Beau before French today, but this time I let him do all the talking.

It was refreshing to be able to be silent and not bored. I learned a lot about him, I learn a lot about him every time I see him. It's refreshing to have someone who doesn't idealize me and yet doesn't hate me. I still don't feel completely real, but maybe that'll fade. I don't know. I've written all these letters to you, and I still don't really know anything. I did do pretty well on my mid-terms though. I got a B on my Psych exam and an A on the paper I had to write for English. There was no mid-term for French, so of course Beau and I celebrated by smoking a bowl and going to the Bourgeois Pig for a game of pool and milkshakes. I don't think you ever got to see the Bourgeois Pig. It's a little café in Silver Lake with a really relaxing atmosphere. You would have loved it.

November 11, 2010

Today is the last day at school before we go on break for Thanksgiving, also I quit Pulse and got a better job at The Village working for Aldo. I got a 50 cent raise on my base pay, plus I'll be making commission on every sale. Of course, Beau and I had to celebrate. He smuggled his bong to school in his backpack, we filled it up in the restroom, and got massively stoned before French today. You'd think going to class high every Thursday would make it hard to focus, but c'est pas vrai. Beau and I are doing pretty well on the tests and we've both been getting As and Bs on the assignments. I'm doing pretty well in Psych also, looks like I'm getting a B- if things continue the way they're going.

The only class I'm irritated with his English 103, because Professor Eriksson is making us wrote a rough draft of a 20-page play and it's due shortly after the break. The play is going to count as our final though, so I really need to put my all into it. Anyway, tonight after class Lily took me to a party. It wasn't a wild, raging, the whole house is upside down kind of party. It was a more sophisticated event. Lily said I needed to go to more parties like that.

"They suit you better," she said.

Anyway, the party was at Alana Salkin's house. I'm not sure if you ever met her, but I'm sure you heard of her. Alana Salkin is legendary. She's rich. She's tall and pretty, and from the stories I heard when we were teenagers, she had the most fun getting into trouble. I actually was nervous to meet her, but once I did, I saw there was no need to be. She's far more down-to-earth than people give her credit for and she's a great hostess. She greeted everyone at the party, literally, no joke. She walked around the house inside and out, hugged the people she knew and gave the people she didn't know her name and shook their hands. This is how I met her. We were standing in the kitchen, Lily and I, and Alana walked right up to Lily and hugged her. Then before Lily could even introduce me, Alana extended her hand and gave me her name.

"Hi, I'm Alana. This is my house, welcome," she said cheerfully.

"Hi, I'm Colin, nice to meet you."

"Hey, I know you from Facebook."

When she said this, I couldn't help but laugh. Social networking has really taken over our lives. "Oh, cool." I tried to say that with just the right amount of enthusiasm as to sound flattered, and not nonchalant. The night wore on and as Alana suggested I helped myself to a mix drink. I looked out the kitchen window. The view was breathtaking. Alan's house is on a hill. It's also fantastically decorated and usually swarming with people dressed brilliantly just to mingle and catch up. Alana disappeared in the crowd and when she came back, she had a bubbler with her. She also had Nathaniel Jacobsen with her – another legend. I happened to know Nathaniel a little more personally. We met because he worked at Pulse for about three months before quitting and going to work for his dad. He didn't want to, but he hated Pulse so much that he ended up choosing the lesser of two evils. We all chatted for a while. Then Alana turned to offer me a hit from her bubbler.

"Thanks," I said "This is going to sound totally lame, but I'm pretty stoked to finally meet you. You're quite a legend."

"Why thank you," she said graciously "Nate here tells me you're quite a legend yourself." You know that cheesy movie moment where the popular girl from high school notices you and suddenly you feel like nothing can touch you, I had that. There we were, Alana, Nathaniel Jacobsen and I standing in Alana's kitchen smoking a bowl. I felt validated. It's kind of silly but given what I've been going through lately it just felt nice. It was different from hanging out with any of my other friends. Maybe it's because Alana and Nate are a couple years older than me and yet we've gone down similar paths. I get to see what I could turn out to be in a couple years. I mean I'm not going to be literally like them that would be impossible.

Alana's mom died when she was 16, her dad died just a few months ago. I won't know what it's like to lose both parents until years from now, if I'm lucky. Nate, who still has both his parents, has a story of his own I don't even know. I keep thinking that I could mature the way they've matured. Alana inherited everything when her dad passed and didn't seem the least bit unappreciative of what she has. Nate says he only parties on the weekends now and wouldn't dream of going into work hung-over. They drink, smoke, indulge, but they create a balance. Nate works as a paralegal and Alana is pursuing acting. I'm sure there's a lot more to their lives than that. I'm sure there are difficulties, but they find a way to make it work. Everyone has their own way of coping.

November 22, 2010

I went to work and when I got off, I noticed a call from Kate. I called her back and she invited me to Thanksgiving dinner at her place. Dad and Faye are going to Ohio to visit some relatives of hers through Christmas. I wouldn't know what to do or how to enjoy a trip to the Midwest even if they had invited me to go with them, which they didn't. Since they're going to be gone, I decided to take Kate's offer. I have nothing to lose I suppose, and I'll get to talk to Parker. I really miss my brother. I wish I hadn't screwed things up with him. In all of the mess that's the one thing I truly regret. He always trusted me. He always looked up to me. He always relied on me, and I used that against him just to one-up Kate. It seems absolutely idiotic now that I've put things into perspective.

November 25, 2010

I woke up early, showered, shaved and picked out clothes for dinner at Kate's. It was cold out, so I wore a light gray scarf with a pale blue button down short, jeans, a blazer and black gloves. I left the house and two hours later I was standing in front of Kate's apartment building. I took a deep breath and entered the lobby. I walked up the same staircase I'd trailed probably a thousand times. Then I was outside of her door, it felt strange knocking. Parker answered and invited me in. The living room was halfway full of people already. Parker's dad was even there.

Parker walked up and hugged me. It was a real whole hug that didn't need any words to follow it. The rest of the people there were Kate's friends, Ms. Foley and Ms. Alleyne were amongst them of course. Ms. Foley was decked out in pearls and wore a shoulder-less black Michael Kors dress. She was of course seated next to Ms. Alleyne who had on a Swarovski crystal leaf necklace, gray laced pom Anna Sui dress with shoulder straps, and a mink stole over it. They each clutched cosmopolitans. They were shimmering, serially single, clichés who had nothing better to do than compare who got the better settlement in their last divorce. They whispered as I walked up to them to say hello. I ignored it, greeted them as politely as possible, then walked away.

Kate made her grand entrance next. She walked in wearing a short cream-colored Nina Ricci dress, Manolo Blahnik heels, and diamond necklace with matching tennis bracelet passed down to her by her mother. Kate was the grand-dame of the night. You would think she was a Caroline Astor based on her outfit and comportment alone, and in her mind she was. She made her way around the living room greeting all her guests, friends and frenemies alike. Then she ushered us all into the kitchen where platters full of food were set up all centered around the great big turkey that Kate named King Henry VIII. It's a little tradition she started, naming the turkey every year. It's always named after a king. Then Kate came over and hugged me. It was private, while everyone was spooning food onto their plates. It felt genuine. I was surprised and relieved and actually a bit happy. Once it was over I started serving myself. I walked over to where Parker was sitting and sat beside him. Kate had left the guests for a brief moment to take a call from Traci.

"Hey," I said. I nudged him with my elbow playfully.

"Hey," he answered. He sounded more somber than I'd expected.

"Look, I'm sorry for tricking you," I said. I figured it was best to dive right into the issue. "I just got caught up in winning this stupid fight with Mom."

"It's okay, I forgive you for that. But I don't forgive you for leaving me here alone with her. Do you know how much she meddles in my life now?" he said. We both laughed and Parker hugged me. That was the best thing that happened the entire evening.

December 6, 2010

I survived working Black Friday at Aldo. In fact, I thrived, if I may say so myself. I made a lot of sales (racking up my commission!) and gave customer service that really impressed my boss. I've received more hours this week because of it. Oh, and school started again last week as well. This week is finals week. I went to Kate's for tea before school Tuesday. It was pleasant. I think in the midst of all the bitterness and battles between us, we were just two people struggling to understand each other. She hurt me for a long time, then I started fighting back, and that didn't help. It just became a vicious cycle.

You prick me, I prick you, we both bleed. I don't want to bleed anymore. I get the feeling she doesn't either. Both of us were wrong at different times. Both of us are to blame and I think we can finally start to build something healthy now that it's all out there. I don't know though, only time will tell. Anyhow, after Psych class today I got text from a co-worker at Pulse. His name is Dominic he's just graduated from some art school and he's heavily into photography. Apparently, he was putting together a portfolio, and he didn't have enough male models. I was honored that he asked me.

"You'd make a great model dude, no homo," he said. How could I not agree? We met up at Griffith Park. It's the perfect place for a photoshoot, I think.

"Just be natural," Dominic said, so I was. I ran around and he took pictures. I was wearing mirrored sunglasses, a light gray James Perse cardigan, a white V-neck shirt, a mahogany scarf, black slim fit jeans, and moccasins that matched the scarf. I ran up to the Griffith J. Griffith statue and wrapped my arms around it loving. I sat in streets and on park benches and stared off into the sky. All the while Dominic snapped pictures. After about an hour and a half we were done. He said he'd send me the photos via email. I have to admit I'm pretty excited about it. It's something new to look forward to.

December 22, 2010

I made it through finals, I won't know what my grades are until a little after New Year's, but I feel like I did pretty well, especially when it came to English 103. The play I wrote was about a 17th century duchess who watches both her parents murdered by her uncle and a short while later, forced to prostitute when her drunkard gambling-addicted brother loses everything they have. Don't worry she has her revenge. It's morbid, I know but you know I've always loved that kind of stuff. You used to love it too if I remember correctly, which I do. God I'm so glad the semester is over! Anyway, today I received the photos from Dominic. The photos came out really well! Everything was done in brilliant color. They trees came alive, the sunlight seemed to burst through in the background, and I looked pretty damn good running around everywhere like a wild child. He's already asked me to do another shoot. He said I could choose any setting and style I wanted, and we'd just go with it.

I'm thinking about doing something edgy, like a punk theme. It'll be me paying homage to the days when all I listened to was Dead Kennedys, Bad Religion, and The Clash. You remember sophomore year at Villa High, don't you? Anyway, I'm excited to get started on that. For now, I have to focus on finals, which are coming up after winter vacation. I'm not really nervous or anything and I don't study much. I don't believe in studying excessively, like cramming. I just read through my notes a couple of times and then go for it. Things have worked out well with that method thus far, so I have no reason to believe it won't continue to work. Oh, by the way Kate invited me to Christmas Eve dinner with Parker's dad's family. It's a bit strange that even though she and Parker's dad are divorced we still go there for Christmas dinner, but it's a tradition. Besides out of all the odd occurrences in my family Christmas with the Lane's is most assuredly the least harmful.

December 26, 2010

Yesterday was Christmas. I woke up in last night's clothes and spent the morning recovering from the hangover I'd acquired on Christmas Eve. I spent Christmas Eve dinner with the Lanes, where everybody drinks imported beer and red wine. They all sit around the television enveloped in deep conversations about their least lucrative business endeavor or calculated career change. Christmas Eve dinner with the Lanes, the most exclusive party you'll never be invited to unless you're born into the dynasty or married into it. And even that doesn't guarantee an invite. Screw up, say the wrong thing, offend the wrong aunt or uncle and you can kiss your place setting at the dinner table goodbye. This family is more traditional and ancient. Kate's upbringing, the antiquated values passed from Eugène to Eugène for generations, primed her to one day become Anderson Lane's wife. The Lane family didn't love that she was Black, but what could they do about it?

Anderson is the first-born son of the third born son. First-born son of the third born son is a meaningless position. Though Anderson's a nice guy his birth order doesn't win him any special notes with the family. Parker is the first born in his entire generation; this makes him golden with the Lanes. It also elevates Anderson a bit for being his dad. What he lacked due to birth order, he regained due to the happy accident of my mother getting pregnant at just the right time. For every family portrait Parker sits at the front of the line with all the offspring born after him, sitting in their birth order behind him. This is what it's like in the Lane family.

I have to admit it's a bit awesome to watch. I'm the older half- brother of the chosen one. It's kind of cool. It's even cooler that this is the one event I get to go to all year where I can take a break from being the center of attention – not that I'm complaining but with all crazy occurrences in my life I think you understand why I enjoy it. At the Lane's no one talks about me, no one gossips, no knows anything other than what Anderson's told them. I spent Christmas Eve eating until I felt stuffed and then walked around with my Belgian beer, chit chatting with different relatives of my brother's until it was time to go. I hated it and I loved it.

Christmas day wasn't as exciting. Kate held another the dinner, it was the same as Thanksgiving, same guests, same ritzy embellishments around the apartment – the only difference was the Christmas tree. Of course, Kate chose to buy a plastic one instead of the real thing, aplastic tree that came with all the lights and bells and ornaments one could ever need packed into a giant white box. Andy came by and brought a little red box with him. In it were more ornaments, only these were special, these had been in his family since forever and some great grand-aunt of his decided it was time to pass them down to Parker.

Kate put them up with pride. Everyone heard about them for the rest of the night. Everyone drank their cosmos and gin and tonics and martinis and wine. Everyone has a good time, yes even me. But it made me miss you and how we used to sneak off and roam the streets together on Christmas day. Kate would always be fuming when she realized I was missing, if she happened to realize. I wish we could do that again. I wish we could climb out of our windows and meet up in front of Villa High, cause a ruckus, cause trouble without getting into the trouble, the way we used to. But we can't.

January 2, 2011

It's a New Year. I decided not to make any resolutions. I didn't want to start off the year by making promises that I probably won't keep. I did however attend Alana Salkin's New Year's Eve bash. I received an invitation from Alana herself via text. It was a masquerade-themed party. Guests were highly advised to dress their best. I decided to wear a Pierre Cardin tuxedo, with black Stacy Adams oxfords. Kate bought the suit for me early last year. The shoes were a gift from Dad. I'd ordered my mask from an online shop and was pleased with the results. It was hand-made, composed of a richly embroidered silver cloth exterior, that was molded over a hard plastic interior. Satin ties looped at each end to secure it to the face.

I went to the party with Lily. Lily's mask was black lace with a big black feather planted on the left side. She was wearing a teal chiffon dress. When we walked into Alana's there was glitter and confetti everywhere and it wasn't even midnight yet. Villa Valle High alumni from classes '07 and '08 (my year) mixed in with a few faces I had never seen before. Scores of people paced throughout the house. Alana made her usual rounds and even changed outfits a couple of times. We all danced, smoked a little pot, and sipped champagne until the clock struck 12. I had a really great time. I didn't feel the need to drink until I pass out or pop any pills. It was refreshing.

January 14, 2011

I worked the day shift at Aldo (which I loved) then I went to Alana's for a wine tasting. I love being on winter break. On the days I don't have work, I can just get up, get out of the house and go wherever I want. Dad is thrilled that I'm being so productive. I'm thrilled that he's proud of me. I still have my fun, but I'm keeping a balance. At Alana's wine tasting I met a girl named Francesca. Francesca is thin and blonde, a bit shorter than me, with emerald-green eyes, and a radiant smile. Yes, she's beautiful but that's not even why I was drawn to her. There was something else about her. She was brazen, yet refined and funny. She walked right up to me while we were all standing around in the family room of the house, talking and sipping the hot cinnamon wine Alana made herself. She walked right up to me and said, "hey remember me," and honestly, I didn't. When this happens and it happens a lot, since, you know I go out a lot, I usually lie and say yes. I say yes just so the other person doesn't feel uncomfortable. But when she asked and I looked into those eyes, those iridescent green eyes, I couldn't lie.

"No, I don't really," I said.

"You don't? We slept together you jerk," she said in a loud whispered.

"I'm sorry," I said. I was searching her face for a sense of familiarity, but nothing. This had never happened to me before. I began grasping at excuses in my mind. I was probably wasted when we hooked up. I had to have been.

"I'm kidding," she interrupted as I had just began spiraling. "My name is Francesca, we haven't sleep together, but we did meet the other night."

"Oh, thank God," I said. I hadn't meant to say it out loud, but my inner brain betrayed my tongue. "Not that you aren't attractive or anything," I stammered. This was not my finest moment by a long shot. I was completely flailing.

"You must get around a lot," she said.

"I wouldn't say that. I'd say I'm experienced," I said. She'd had me on the ropes at our introduction, but I felt I had made a smooth recovery with this statement.

"Experienced is just a fancy way of saying you've been around. But you're kind of cute, so I don't mind," she said. She smiled when she said it. I have always been a sucker for a beautiful smile.

"Just kind of cute?" I replied. I felt all trepidation leave my body. I was back in the game. We spent a couple of hours chatting about music, novels, and poetry we'd read after that. I discovered that we shared a passion for the works of Anais Nin, Oscar Wilde, and Sylvia Plath. I also found out she's quite athletic. She enjoys hang-gliding, rock climbing, and waterskiing. She's also traveled quite a bit and wants to do so even more (something else we have in common). So, she's beautiful and smart and funny but not in the least bit arrogant or shallow. Her sister is her best friend. Her parents are always either working or travelling, so they're not very close, but she loves them none-the-less. I know I don't know her very well yet, but I just got a good feeling from being around her. I definitely want to see her again.

January 30, 2011

I went to an acting workshop at Alana's house tonight after work. I haven't thought about acting in years, but I couldn't say no. Alana was so sweet when she asked, and Lily joined in to convince me. Lily drove me there. I texted Francesca during the car ride. We've been talking a lot lately. I found out she's my age and is also attending Villa Community College. I've been resolute not to get too close to her or anyone else, but she's quickly slipping past my defenses. Her wit, charm, and cute little laugh are all too beguiling. She's frank and prudent at all the right times.

These past few weeks, we had a more in-depth discussion about our favorite hobbies and shared stories of some of our most embarrassing mistakes. She's really unconventional. Almost nothing shocks her. I'm far more into her than I'd ever admit, unless she asks. God, I'm an idiot. I swore I wouldn't fall for anyone again and here I am falling for Francesca. Anyhow, the workshop went great. Everyone had to read a monologue. When it was my turn, I realized I forgot to bring a monologue with me. Luckily, I happened to have the rough draft of a play I wrote for my English 103 class, in the notebook I used to take on everyone else's readings.

The crowd loved my reading. I was flattered as I hadn't acted in years, but especially because I was amongst theater school graduates who were actively working in the industry. Some of Alana's friends were booking commercials, sitcom appearances, and soap opera debuts. Maybe they weren't famous yet, but they were hitting the ground running. Lily mentioned how great my writing was. She asked if I wanted to make a short film together.

There's this local film festival holding a contest where the grand-prize is $5,000 in cash and a live premiere of the work in question. I'd be responsible for the script, and she'd direct it. I know she'd make a great director. I just don't know that I have the juice to write a short film.

"It's judged by a panel of legit film critics. It's not even about the money, it's about getting out there," Lily said. "We can cast Alana and the actors here."

I'm definitely going to consider it. Aside from that I've been spending more time with Kate. Things have been going swimmingly with us, save a few casual disagreements. She's really trying. I'm really trying, and we're making progress. Parker and I have pretty much been back to normal since after Thanksgiving. Traci even called me!

February 14, 2011

I've been spending more time alone lately. I still enjoy going out, but I've realized I use socializing as a means to avoid being alone with my thoughts. I've decided to face solitude head on, rather than continue run from it, except for today that is. Today was Valentine's Day and I spent it with Francesca. I guess you could call it a date. We went to lunch at the Cheesecake Factory in Pasadena. We both didn't want to make a big deal about the holiday but didn't want to stay inside either. We agreed to treat it just like any other day and save ourselves the spectacle. It was rather relaxing. We got to know each other even better. I discovered she's a Philosophy major and works at an art supplies store. She really wants to be a teacher. She learned that I'm a Poli Sci major and have no idea what I want to do with that.

We both find the smell of lilac overbearing and like The Strokes. It was going well, and we weren't thinking about the fact that it was Valentine's Day at all, until our server asked if we wanted the dessert special. Francesca made a gagging face that was still cute as hell, and I politely told him it wouldn't be necessary. We ate and since the subject was already on the table, we discussed some of our past Valentine's Days. The best Valentine's Day for her was seventh grade when a kid named Bobby Sherman left candy and a note that said 'be mine' at her seat in second period. Her worst Valentine's Day was the same year, when she realized Bobby Sherman mixed her seat up with another girl's. It was a simple mistake on Bobby's part. Francesca and the other girl sat right next to each other. Unfortunately, Francesca had already written a note back and passed it to him.

"Imagine my humiliation," she said laughing.

The best Valentine's Day for me was sophomore year in high school when I went to the dance with Amelia. She came over to Kate's all dressed up. Neither of them stopped smiling or chatting for what seemed like hours, while we waited for Kate to finish getting ready so she could drop us off. Kate's been fond of Amelia ever since.

My worst Valentine's Day was pretty much everyone after that. Francesca laughed when I said that. We walked around Old Town Pasadena after we finished lunch. Today is definitely a candidate for the Best Valentine's Day column. Oh, and I agreed to do the short-film with Lily. We're going to start this summer.

February 23, 2011

Francesca and I have been growing dangerously close as of late. We haven't slept together yet. We're taking it slow and surprisingly I'm loving it. It's wonderfully refreshing to spend time with someone, without any expectations. We had a moment last weekend though and I'm not quite sure what to make of it. We were at one of Alana's house parties. We all drank and played Cranium. We were drunk, but not blackout drunk (I've taken a break from imbibing so heavily as of late). Francesca and I wound up on the same team. We pretty much dominated the entire game except for the section where we had to draw blue cards. Damn those blue cards.

Anyway, after a few rounds of the game, we made our way to Alana's backyard so we could be alone together. We stood dressed in warm winter clothes, drunk, and swaying. Careful to keep our distance from the massive pool behind us, we leaned against the guardrails and took in the sweeping view of the city from the hillside. I took Francesca's hand in mine and told her she was just as gorgeous as the view.

"Really?" she asked.

"Actually no," I said abruptly.

"You're such a dick," she said. Her jaw dropped in comic disbelief. She laughed and nudged me with her elbow.

"You're more gorgeous than it," I said in response.

"Ok Casanova," she said mockingly. She moved in closer, and I wrapped my arms around her. We kissed sweet kisses under the stars. It was cheesy but romantic in all the right ways. It felt perfect.

"You know in moments where everything just feels right, like now? I always hear specific songs in my head. Almost like a soundtrack to what's going on in my life. It sounds corny, but do you ever have moments like that?" she asked.

"I have them all the time," I shouted. We stayed there together for a while and joked about eloping. The jokes turned into what sounded like a semi-serious conversation. It's completely illogical, but also why not?

March 19, 2011

I have so much to tell you. I don't even know where to begin. I guess I should start by saying that Francesca and I decided to call it quits. We were on the same page until last Sunday. We talked immediately following Alana's last party and agreed that the wedding fantasy jokes were just that jokes. We let ourselves get too drunk and carried away. No harm was done. We laughed it off and kept seeing each other.

Last Sunday started out like any other day. I woke up early and got dressed to *Come on Eileen* by Dexy's Midnight Runners. Dad and Faye were already at work, so I left the house without issue. I hummed the song as I made my way to the train station and two hours later, I was back in Villa Valle. Francesca and I were texting back and forth during my journey. She said she would be St. George's Parish attending mass and asked if I wanted to meet after. The church was only a few blocks away, so I readily agreed.

By the time I made it to St. George's, Francesca was on the steps outside. I could tell something was off by her demeanor. Still, I gave her a hug and s kiss on the forehead. She sniffed my neck and asked what cologne I was wearing. I'd put on Polo by Ralph Lauren to draw her in, but pretended I couldn't recall the scent. I asked if she wanted to grab a bite to eat and that's when she blurted out that she wasn't over her ex. I was instantaneously annoyed. I thought about all the time I had invested in getting to know her, when I could have been seeing someone who had a real interest in building a relationship with me.

I sat on the steps of St. George's Parish and heard her out. When she was done, I thanked her for her honesty and rose to leave. I realized that I hadn't taken the time to process my experiences with dating for the past three years. I was still hung up on Leona when I started hooking up with Alessandra. My fling with Alessandra had barely dissolved, before I started seeing Chloe. I dated Gisele then practically dated

Duncan immediately after, and now I was here with Francesca. Could I honestly say I was ready to make a clean break? Francesca seemed bewildered as I rose to leave. She reached out and grabbed my arm to stop me. "Can we at least still be friends?" she asked.

"Let's not kid ourselves," I said. She hadn't done anything wrong, but I'm no fool. I've been in her position before. I knew we weren't really going to be friends. Why play the game? I was ready to cut ties. If my past experiences taught me anything, it's that I wasn't the type to launch into a friendship with a romantic interest. I need time to recalibrate. It's unhealthy to force yourself to turn feelings off and we don't owe everyone our friendship. Sometimes you try to make a go of dating, and it doesn't pan out. It's okay to say goodbye and move on. I find that we ask to be friends in situations like this, when what we really mean is, 'can we be friendly?'

"What's that supposed to mean?" she said. Her voice quivered and I realized I had upset her. I hadn't wanted this to spiral into an argument. I started to walk away.

"I think we both have enough friends already," I said. I traversed the front steps of the parish and headed down the street. She didn't say anything in return, and I didn't turn back to look at her. I did however realize that I needed to confront my own unresolved issues, if I ever wanted to have a healthy relationship with anyone again. I decided to call Leona the next day. The conversation went alright. I was starting to feel good about things again when Duncan showed up. I had finished my shift at Aldo, when I ran into him. *What fresh hell is this?* I thought to myself. He said hi, I waved, and he sidled up beside me as I tried to make a polite escape.

"Colin, can I talk to you?" he said.

"Sure, but I don't have to listen," I said. The words just flowed out. I was surprised at how upset I was. There was a peaceful resolution to what happened between us or didn't happen in my mind. I had gone through all the stages of grief until I had reached acceptance. There he was ruining all of it, just by existing.

"Colin, come on, we really need to talk," he said.

"Didn't we talk already? I thought you were leaving for the Marines?"

"We didn't really get to talk though, and I am leaving at the end of this month."

"Then why are you wasting your time talking to me? Go celebrate!"

"Typical. You're being closed off as a defense mechanism." He was right and I hated it. I had opened the floodgates to healing old wounds, when I reached out to Leona. I figured it only made sense to hear Duncan out.

"Alright, let's talk," I said. We talked about everything you could think of. We discussed his feelings, my feelings, and the disconnect between the two of us. I realized in the midst of all this talking that a lot had changed. I didn't really want or need anything from him. I had figured him out. I knew how unreliable he was. I knew he cared about me in some strange way, but that wasn't enough. He wasn't secure. He wasn't ready to be with anyone, least of all me. He was into the idea of being with me, but his crush was never going to materialize into meaningful action. In the time we've known each other, we've shared a kiss here and there, or a hug that lasted a little too long, but nothing deeply tangible.

"I'm sorry, but I'm not going to let you do this again," I said.

"Do what again?" He asked.

"Dive into my life, just so you can dive right out again. I get it you isolate yourself when you can't handle life. You can't expect your friends and lovers to be waiting for you when you want to come back to us. Life doesn't stop for anybody." I hadn't meant to quote The Perks of Being a Wallflower, but it felt apt.

"I don't get another chance?" he asked. His eyes darted back and forth across my face. He was searching for a modicum of hope, no doubt. I didn't deliver.

"This would be the second time you were given a second chance," I said.

"You know Peter denied Jesus three times and Jesus still loved him," he said. I knew there was genuine emotion tied to these words. His protestant upbringing had unwittingly made an appearance.

"Yeah, but I'm not Jesus," I said. "Take care." I walked away and felt the most powerful feeling. It was a feeling I haven't felt in a long while. I was proud of myself.

June 16, 2011

I know haven't written you in a while. I've been trying to figure out how to conclude this all. I suppose I start should by saying that this will be my last letter to you. I'm grateful to have done this. I needed to mull over the details of my thus far, largely vapid existence. I needed to be frank with you, if no one else. You always listened and understood. You never passed judgement in a way that felt critical, yet you always gave me your honest opinion. I regret that I never got the chance to apologize for how uneven our friendship was. I'm sorry I was too self-indulgent to really be a friend to you. I always thought that if I had known how much pain you were in, I would have figured out a way to save you somehow. Now, I know better.

You played great music. You were always talking about some good new book you read, or some play you'd seen. I couldn't believe it when your parents told Will and me what happened to you. I've never known anyone who'd committed suicide before. I'd never known anyone who had been shot, let alone shot themselves. More importantly, I never knew you were so deeply despondent. Your funeral was surreal (you would have hated it, looking back). I guess that's when I first started falling apart. You were always there for me. I wish you were still here now so I could be there for you this time around.

I can only imagine how difficult it must've been for you to go to a private school so out of town. I bet it must've been infuriating for you to help me solve my ridiculous problems, all the while no one knowing how hurt, sad, and in need of help you were. But I digress, this is about honoring you. It'll be two years since you've been gone next this coming fall. I'll never forget the day – September 24, 2007. You were such an amazing friend. I needed you to know about all the things you missed. I needed you to know that I finally get it. My worth isn't determined by material possessions, sexual attractiveness, or social standing.

Life isn't about collecting clothes, conquests, or approval from the in-crowd. Life is about making something of ourselves. It's about doing something meaningful, touching someone's life in an impactful way, and being present to enjoy the good times. I've made some colossal mistakes, but I regret nothing. Every error has taught me something valuable. If you were still here, I'd have had no choice but to be as honest with you in person, as I was in these letters. I'm certain that with patience and therapy, I can find that guidance on my own.

For the longest time after you passed away, I didn't know how to bounce back. I thought I had it, but I realize now I just buried it all with drinking, drugs, sex – anything to fill the void. Now I'm getting stronger and stronger every day. I know myself a lot better than I did when we first met. I'm still not perfect by any stretch of the imagination, but I'm improving. I'm trying to do everything in moderation. I'm proud of myself and I know you'd be proud of me too. This is goodbye, but I won't forget you. I'll visit the cemetery to see you tomorrow. Will has already agreed to go with me. I know neither of us has been to visit in a while.

After we visit, we're heading to Monterrey. Will's family has a house there and they're letting us use it to shoot that short-film Lily was talking about. I finished writing the story a few days ago. It's a re-telling of the last two years of my life. All the chaos I've written to you about in these letters. It's been fictionalized a bit, but I think it's still true enough to form. Leo, Ezra, and Alana are going to play themselves and a small group of Alana's friends have been cast to fill the other roles. I'm nervous to see my story ...I mean Henry's story unfold. Henry Walcott is the main character's name. I won't be exploring Paris or London, like you and I used to talk about, but it's something. It's a new leaf. I feel like I'm finally starting to live up to my potential. I'll be gone for a month. My boss says my job will be waiting when I get back. So, that's it. I'm off to embark on this new adventure. Thanks for everything.

All my love,

CP

ABOUT THE AUTHOR

Hayden Winston is a Black, bisexual, novelist, poet, and activist. He holds a BSc in Criminal Justice and a Master of Legal Studies. His work draws on his experiences growing up in Los Angeles as a QPOC and the child of West Indian immigrants. He currently resides in Northern California, with his husband and their two cattle dogs.

In Last Night's Clothes was his debut novel and first self-published work. He went on to self-publish two poetry chapbooks, *Les Saisons* and *Bellator ego sum*. His second novel, *Wildflowers* was published by Nine Star Press in the summer of 2021.